T0354334

ATHENA

A NOVEL

Elizabeth Fritz

iUniverse, Inc.
New York   Bloomington

Athena

iUniverse books may be ordered through booksellers or by contacting:

iUniverse
1663 Liberty Drive
Bloomington, IN 47403
www.iuniverse.com
1-800-Authors (1-800-288-4677)

ISBN: 978-1-4401-3489-0 (pbk)
ISBN: 978-1-4401-3488-3 (ebk)

Printed in the United States of America

iUniverse rev. date: 4/13/2009

Also by Elizabeth Fritz

Surprise! Surprise!

Cousin Delia's Legacy

Hope's Journey

Trio

Assisted Living—Or Dying?

Dedicated to friends and family
who enjoy my books

1

The amber neon of Bigby's Pharmacy threw golden light across the parking lot and painted my beloved white Prius a glowing yellow. As I inserted my key into the door, my mind reveled in the car's gleaming perfection and the pleasurable prospect of driving it to the new job I would start in the morning. In an instant everything changed. Without warning a beefy man in dark clothes and wearing a ski mask loomed up beside me. He grabbed at my hand and before I knew it, I was flat on the pavement, dazed and voiceless from the suddenness and ferocity of his attack, stunned as my head hit the asphalt. Barely aware that the attacker had opened the door and thrown himself into the driver's seat, I heard the engine start and the car roar off at full speed. But I was more aware that in the process the car had run over my left leg, cast and all. Drowning in a red blur of excruciating pain I was thinking: Damn it, if not for that cast I could run after that guy and reclaim my car. From the edge of consciousness I heard a scream of skidding tires, the crash and crunch of crumpling metal, and the tinkle of shattering glass. My next impression was Mrs. Bigby bending over me, struggling to push her wadded-up apron under my head. The apron smelled of peppermint. Her kindly old face a mask of distress, she was saying, "It's all right, honey; the mister is calling the police. Are you hurt?"

A bulky figure in red and black flannel knelt on the other side,. Darkness and the bill of a baseball cap veiled his features. I realized that his was the warm grasp that engulfed my hand and I made an effort to raise myself from the ground. But all I could think of aside from my pain was my car.

"My car, my car," I sobbed. "It's almost new, just 297 miles on the odometer. What's happened to it?" Then as the pain in my leg swelled to a new crescendo, I babbled, "He ran over my leg, broke it all over again, I'll never get to my new job tomorrow. Car wrecked, leg smashed, Oh God!"

"Don't worry about it," the big man soothed. "EMS is on the way. The carjacker ran head-on into my car and got out and ran. I stayed with my car long enough to talk to On*Star, then I saw you were down and had them send help. By the time I got untangled from my airbag, the guy was long gone. The cops just got here. Now, try not to fuss and maybe it won't hurt so bad."

"My purse," I mumbled, "my purse was on the front seat."

"I'll try to find it and get it to you...."

His voice faded away into a mist where EMS must have packed me up and hauled me off to the hospital, because the next thing I knew I was in a curtained cubicle with a saline drip stuck to the back of my right hand. A big man in a red and black plaid flannel shirt was sitting in a nearby visitor chair and holding my purse on his lap. It had to be the man from the accident. I struggled to get my eyes in focus. The man was maybe thirty-five, forty years old, with bushy black hair and a unkempt beard streaked with gray, sharp gray eyes, an outdoor complexion, and a burly build that dwarfed the spindly chair he occupied.

"Who are you?" I mumbled. "Where did you find my purse? What are you doing here?"

"I thought you needed to have someone with you. Your purse was on the front seat of your car. I told the cops I was your brother and brought the purse along when I snagged a ride in the ambulance. I figured it had your ID and insurance cards and so forth and you would need it."

"I don't have a brother," I said in wonder. "I don't even know anybody in Avalon. I just moved here a week ago. I'm supposed to start a new job tomorrow morning."

As I rambled, the white curtain parted to admit a slender Asian in a white coat. "I'm Dr. Soo," he said, his voice as gentle as his touch on my hand. "I'm going to examine you for scrapes and bruises and a possible concussion. I checked your leg while you were still unconscious and decided I needed to call in your orthopedist as soon as possible. If you'll give me his name, the nurse will contact him while I examine you."

Although my perceptions were fuzzy, I tried to rise to the occasion without whining as I strained to remember a name. "I just moved to Avalon a week ago. I have a referral from my former doctor. But I haven't seen the new doctor yet. Oh, now I remember, his name is MacLaren, Brian MacLaren."

"Is it OK with you if I turn you over to him as soon as he gets here? You will certainly need his attention and if you have any records of the previous injury he will want them." Turning to the man in the flannel shirt, Dr. Soo inquired, "And who are you?"

The big man rose and introduced himself, "I'm an imposter, Doctor. I told the emergency services I was this young lady's brother so I would be allowed to see her safely to medical care. My name is Eric Harald and when you throw me out, I will leave my address and phone numbers at the desk, hoping that the young lady will let me know how she gets along. This is her purse."

At a gesture from the doctor, Mr. Harald left the purse by my side on the cot, dropped a comforting pat on my hand, and departed through the curtain. A nurse carrying a clipboard chart appeared to take care of paper work and valuables and Dr. Soo examined me and ordered a bunch of tests. His orders led to a lot of hauling around in and out of vast machines and had me hurting like the devil. No medicine for pain I was told, until Dr. MacLaren sees you. When asked if I took any medications, I referred the nurse to the Bigbys and the prescription they had just had filled for me; I couldn't recall the name of the pills except there were a lot of Zs and Ps in it.

I lay in a pain-filled stupor until Dr. MacLaren arrived. He was a rotund little man, exuding so much good will and good nature that I readily confided myself to his competence. As he pondered the X-rays, he meditatively rubbed the shining dome of his shaven skull. My muddled brain occupied itself with the way the lights of the examining room reflected on the bare skin. Carefully, piece by piece, he peeled off the crushed remnants of the old cast. His voice was cheerful as he delivered the initial assessment of the damages.

"Your medical-surgical record arrived at my office from Dr. Kastner several days ago. And a good thing, too. I find the pins that Dr. Kastner put in the tibia and fibula are still in place—that's the good news. The bad news is that I'll have to go in and tighten them up and you will have to put up with painful swelling, a new cast, and intensive rehab for at least another month. I'll schedule surgery for tomorrow morning. Who shall we notify to come be with you?"

"There's no one. I moved here a week ago, I'm living in a motel room, I don't know anyone here." I babbled, swallowing hard to stifle the whimpering that waves of pain forced upon my consciousness. "My only contact in this town is the Human Services Director at Nature Productions and she expects me to start work tomorrow morning. My mother is my only surviving family member and she is not free to come."

Weak tears rose and flowed from my eyes. I had fended for myself for years and feeling sorry for myself now was not natural. But I knew in my current predicament I needed help. "Is there someone, maybe a special duty nurse, who can stand by during the surgery and see me out of it?" I asked.

Dr. MacLaren promised a social worker would visit with me before surgery and stay on my case afterwards. Finally the nurse with the clipboard injected a painkiller into the I.V. and in a few minutes blessed relief permeated my battered body. The last thing I remembered then was the clock on the wall with its hands at 11 minutes past 3.

2

The next two days passed in a haze of pain and sedation. The promised social worker had spent half an hour with me and filled out reams of forms before surgery, but then disappeared until I returned to the land of the sentient on Wednesday. She was a plump Latina, soft brown eyes, black hair, cheerful and kind; her name was Miguelita Sanchez but Lita for short. She puzzled for a moment over my name,

"Athena Bonham, is that a Greek name? It's very pretty."

I reeled off a lie that I had practiced for years: that my father, a classical scholar, had hoped he was endowing me with wisdom by naming me for Athena, the Greek goddess of wisdom. In fact, the line for "father" on my birth certificate was blank. Since paternal DNA was all I had ever had of him, I felt I was at liberty to invent whatever kind of father I chose. It made people comfortable to assume I had one and in moments of introspection, it made me comfortable too.

Lita had gone to my motel, packed up my things, and paid my bill with my credit card. She stowed my luggage in her office at the hospital. She had also called Nature Productions, explained my situation, and wrung a promise from the Director of Human Services to keep the position open for another month. "What kind of work do you do?" she wondered. "That woman was kinda snippy."

I explained that I wrote science texts and edited nature films. When Lita asked delicately whether I could weather a period of unemployment while my leg was healing, I assured her without going into detail that I had adequate resources. Those resources stemmed from an indemnity for the initial injury. A careless boom operator had lowered his boom on me when I was working on location for a studio making a natural history epic. The studio preferred to settle for a tidy $250,000 rather than face a claim against its insurance.

But I had more pressing insurance issues to settle, namely my car. I called the local agent and got his report. Totaled, he said; he had gone to the impound lot and cleared out personal possessions which he delivered to me in a plastic grocery bag. I could have cried. That little car was my dream car. The only way to deal with its demise was simply to buy a replacement—which I would do as soon as I could get around on my own again. On Thursday the police interviewed me and told me there was very little chance the carjacker would be identified and caught. The news increased my depression. During the few days I had already spent looking for lodging in Avalon, I had been charmed by well-kept houses lined up on tree-shaded streets and small but bustling businesses on Main Street. The population was barely 100,000 and the town perched on the wooded banks of the scenic Blue Fox River, surrounded by rich farm fields and prosperous farmsteads. I had expected to be happy settled here. My injury was healed and my financial situation was very good. But now optimism was giving way to dark thoughts.

Pain was eased somewhat by Miguelita's brief daily visits. Then a different visitor appeared—Mr. Harald lugging a mammoth pot of bronze chrysanthemums. I got my first good look at him and decided he was quite a handsome man. Now clean shaven and skillfully barbered, he displayed a firm jaw, well-defined cheekbones, and an imposing brow. In his trim business suit he seemed taller and more slender than I recalled from my first impression. I confessed he didn't seem the same person I remembered wearing a flannel jacket and sitting in the visitor chair of the emergency room cubicle. He laughed and explained. "The night of your accident I was on my way home from two weeks cruising lumber in the north woods and was in desperate need of serious grooming. I hope you find my appearance more conventional today than then."

As we talked I became very conscious of my own appearance. I knew that my black eye had become a revolting purple with green edges and that a touch of lipstick had not redeemed the crusty scrape on my cheek. But his manner put me at ease and we fell effortlessly into a friendly conversation. He insisted I call him Eric when I thanked him repeatedly for his assistance the night of the wreck and asked after his car. He laughed again and reassured me. "It's a Hummer, next thing to a tank. It suffered very little compared to your car. I was sorry to hear about your car; they said it was totaled."

I told him the insurance would cover a new one as soon as I could get out and about, and he volunteered to drive me around to the dealers when I was ready. Over the next four weeks, he repeated his visits every day or so, frequently bringing a cheer-up gift: flowers, magazines, or candy. A stubborn infection was keeping me in bed much of the time and under treatment. Inactivity, Eric's candy, and hospital starch was putting on pounds. I was up with a walker and could examine myself in the bathroom mirror. Once the black eye had reached the light green and yellow stage, and the abrasion on my cheek had faded, with makeup I didn't look so bad. I became less self conscious about my appearance and turned my efforts to mastering the canes and walkers now essential to my mobility.

Although flattered and pleased at Eric's interest in my well-being, I was puzzled by it. I wondered what I had done to deserve such assiduous attention from a complete stranger. Finally, I decided to try some tactful probing. I started by countering his repeated offer to drive me to pick out a car by saying that was very kind but I didn't want to take him away from his family. He caught on right away that I was fishing for background and responded generously.

"My family consists of two teenagers: Dora is 16, beautiful and smart; Don is 15, handsome and consumed by sports. We live in a big house on 30 country acres and I run my business—I'm a broker for lumber and wood products—from the house. My wife passed away two years ago and the three of us have more or less adjusted ourselves to her loss. I should mention that the family includes a live-in housekeeper, her husband who tends to outdoor work, two horses, three Labrador retrievers, three cats and a superfluous kitten, a cockatoo with an astounding vocabulary, and a tortoise who lives in a flower bed. Life is continually busy and noisy, but we like it. But tell me," he went on, "what are you going to do when you're released from the hospital? You won't be able to be on your own for a while."

"Lita suggests an assisted living suite. I've called around to several places but I confess I'm shocked at the prices. Nevertheless, one does what one must."

"Good philosophy, bad economy. I've got an idea. In these past weeks our acquaintance has progressed into friendship, hasn't it? Well, Thena, I've got a guest house on my place, all amenities laid on, and help on tap whenever you might need it. Once you have your car, the doctor's office, the rehab clinic, and a grocery will be in reach. I sometimes rent the guest house to friends, $300 a month. Would you like to look at it?"

I wasn't surprised at his offer so much as I was bewildered. Might this really nice guy, with his unsolicited benevolence, have ulterior motives? He immediately sensed my hesitation. "If you want references, talk to Ben Avery, the hospital administrator. I'm on the Board of Trustees here."

I said thanks and I'd think about it. So the first day that I was allowed to walk with a cane, I hunted up the administrator's office and pursued those references. "Pillar of the community" and "man of honor" were the descriptive phrases. I decided to look at Eric's guest house and on his next visit he drove me to inspect the Harald spread.

The main house and its outbuildings stood in a large clearing at the end of a drive that curved through a wooded area. The single story of the main house, which I guessed was Prairie Style, sprawled over a hill of landscaped terraces and overlooked the countryside through walls of windows. The guesthouse, of similar design and also with lots of windows, stood on a spur of the drive behind a screen of evergreens some 50 yards from the main house. As Eric drove into the spur, three golden retrievers erupted barking and gamboling in greeting from a large barn at the end of the drive. One although elderly, his muzzle bleached with age and his joints stiffened by arthritis, sported gallantly among his young companions. Eric drew up the car before the door of the guest house and scurried around to assist me and my cane on to the porch steps. The dogs sat down in an attentive row to observe.

Eric threw open the handsomely paneled door and we entered a small but elegant foyer. From the foyer, a wide arch opened on a huge living room, a 15-foot ceiling, massive fieldstone fireplace, casual modern furniture dressed in brilliant fabrics, and daylight blazing in through large southeast-facing windows. Eric did something at a panel on the wall and gauzy bamboo shades slowly traveled down from valances to mute the light. Eric indicated with a gesture an informal dining area at one end that led into a small but complete kitchen. The windows that wrapped around from the front to the back of the building provided a near vista of a wooded slope down to a little valley and brook, and more distant wide-angle views of grassy meadows and rolling hills studded with copses of mature trees. From the kitchen, a door led to a spacious deck furnished with sturdy teak benches, chairs, and tables. Two roomy bedrooms, each with its own bathroom, opened from the back hall. Eric flung open an unobtrusive door with a flourish to disclose laundry equipment and mop and broom storage. This guest house wasn't a dolls' house by any means. It also should rent for more than $300 a month, and I said so.

"If that's all you're charging me, I'm insulted. I want you to know I'm not a charity case!"

"Hey, lady," Eric retorted. "And I want *you* to know I'm not some slum lord out to screw my tenants. When I loan this place to my friends, I collect enough to pay for the utilities, that's all."

"It's all so beautifully furnished. Those paintings and sketches and those animal sculptures are outstanding—feasts for the eyes, genuine art objects."

A momentary cloud formed on Eric's face before he responded. "The trimmings were Mary's doing. She collected things like that and when she decided they were clutter in the big house she moved them out here. The running horse and the egret were favorite pieces of hers."

I could understand. The wooden horse had been carved to float on the wind without apparent support and the bird, a contemporary rendering in burnt steel, poised to pounce on the frog at his feet, was true to nature and art at the same time. I knew I would love to live with Mary's "trimmings." I wanted to yield to impulse and take Eric's offer on the spot, but the last time I had acted on impulse had not been a success. He drove me back to the hospital and saw me to my room. I said I'd call him.

3

The next day my conference with Dr. MacLaren left me very thoughtful. He began by reviewing my treatment which by now had included two more surgeries to get bones straight and repeated irrigation of the wounds to conquer a stubborn infection. He was ready to release me from hospital care and would arrange for a rehabilitation program as soon as I had a car. He specified once-a-month evaluations for at least six months and explained why; the infection and its effects still lurked and the damage to the bones of my left leg was permanent. Even when the healing process was complete, I would limp and probably need a cane. Hiking, jogging, walking, standing for any length of time, and ballroom dancing were out. He told me I would not realize the extent of my disability until I tried to resume my former life style. His cautions tipped my decision in favor of a stay in Eric's guest house for at least six months.

I called a taxi and headed to the Toyota agency to scope out the Prius situation. Orders were backed up but the dealer, citing so much recent bad luck and a handicap besides, put me on priority one. That word "handicap" hit hard; until I heard it used, I wasn't aware how others viewed my limp. Was handicap a label I had to learn to live with? I cringed at the thought, then relegated it to the back of my mind. When I got back to my bed at the hospital, I had been to the bank and to the insurance office too. I had a promise of delivery of a car within the week. Exhaustion due to my day's activity brought home how tenuous my strength was. I called and left a message for Eric that I would take his guest house if his offer was still good. I had two days to wait until he was in town again and called me. I spent those two days thinking and thinking hard.

My primary decision was a firm resolve never to whine, never to feel sorry for myself, never to seek a shoulder to cry on. I would, however, accept an arm to lean on when and if I found support absolutely necessary. Foolish pride and misplaced ego make good fodder for movie scenarios and book plots but not for a way of life. I had to work to be as self-sufficient from now on as I had been so far. I barely remembered my mother; she had gone out of my life when I was eight, leaving me with one of her friends in foster care. To my mind I wasn't really in foster care, just "staying with Aunt Julie" and supported with adequate but meager funds from an unknown source. However, by the time I was sixteen I was asking hard questions. Aunt Julie referred me to another friend of my mother, Uncle George Dempsey, a lawyer who sat me down on my sixteenth birthday to put me wise to my situation.

Uncle George was blunt. He was my legal guardian appointed by the court when my mother was sent to serve a life sentence in an institution for the criminally insane. To my anguished question Why?, Uncle George replied with an unvarnished tale of the random murders of a whole family while out of her mind on drugs. Horrified, heartsick, I heard the story and then closed my memory on it. I didn't learn the details until I was old enough and courageous enough to gain access to the trial transcript. Then I accepted her tortured existence but put her out of mind entirely. I knew where she was incarcerated and knew that she neither remembered nor cared about me. Aid to Dependent Children got me through high school and I departed unregretting and unregretted from Aunt Julie's house. Although she had never displayed affection for me, she had done her Christian duty to rear me clean and decent physically and morally. A high school counselor helped me explore scholarship opportunities and I landed a grant to full tuition and board at a small college in a country town. Part-time jobs and strict economy saw me through to a bachelor's degree with a major in Biology, a minor in Art, and a teaching certificate in Elementary Education. In my senior year, my fellow students elected me Homecoming Queen.

I have to confess that my ego willingly and secretly approved of my physical attributes: height five seven, measurements 36-26-36, long graceful legs, a mane of naturally curling naturally blonde hair, long-lashed brown eyes. But the year I did my practice teaching, my mentor advised me that as a second grade school teacher my attributes would best be concealed by clunky clothes, a braid, and horn-rimmed glasses. I was 22 years old when I landed my first teaching job and I stuck with it for four years, more or less content, but vaguely yearning for wider though still undefined horizons.

On impulse I answered a classified ad. *"Interested in adventure? Qualified biologist wanted. Generous salary and benefits."* My answer brought an invitation to an interview with Thad Novak, an experienced movie maker who pretended to be a naturalist. I didn't know it at the time but what he wanted was a decorative female to spice up jungle scenes he shot in exotic venues. I was decorative enough; those blonde tresses, peach-blow complexion, and starlet's figure were just what Thad was looking for. The audition consisted of a reluctant stroll in a bathing suit in front of Thad's camera. I was more comfortable when asked to display my ability to pronounce a vocabulary of scientific names correctly. The salary was indeed generous, especially when compared to my teacher's pay. I accepted the job and got set for a life of adventure. During the first year with Thad, dressed in adequate albeit brief safari clothes, I faced a Sumatran tiger, cuddled a 15-foot anaconda, caressed a fractious meerkat, outraced a hungry cheetah, and survived. Then Thad hauled out a leopard-skin loincloth and handed me a choice—more skin or no paycheck. I got a release from my contract by threatening to report Thad to the vice squad. Nevertheless, the experience with him had not been all bad. I had met several legitimate publishers and movie producers whose work I admired and who were interested in my ability to contribute intellectually to nature presentations.

For two years I worked for Wahl EcoProductions as a scriptwriter and film editor. My work took me to Africa, South America, Melanesia, and Siberia. The accident that smashed my left ankle occurred in backwoods Borneo. Much of the long-term damage was due to a torturous and prolonged trip down a jungle river to competent medical care. By the time a surgeon was patching me up in an Australian hospital, I was also being treated for both jungle rot on my other foot and a case of malaria.

Five months later, still in a cast, I found a desk job advertised at Nature Productions in Avalon, Ohio; I was reasonably healthy again and ready to get back to work. Now this second injury meant I would be obliged to call Nature Productions and tell the snippy Human Resources Director I wasn't available for the position after all. I made up my mind to devote my financial resources and full time to rehabilitation and recovering my ruined health. Unable to hold a job, and needing to stretch my dollars during my recovery, I saw living in Eric's guest house as an opportunity. It would give me a country landscape rich in nature subjects for paintings and sketches. Connections I had made during my association with Wahl EcoProductions would provide access to a potential market for them.

4

The day of my release from the hospital finally came. Lita helped with the paper work. Thank goodness, my insurance had held out through the thousands of dollars racked up by surgeries and hospital stays and would continue for rehab and doctor visits. A nurse came along to my room and loaded the contents of the bedside stand into a big plastic bag. When I rebelled against inclusion of the emesis basin and bed pan, both plastic, she laughed and said, "You got to take 'em. They're bought and paid for. Take 'em home and plant flowers in 'em. Recycling is good."

Lita cleared out the luggage she was keeping in her office and deposited it and me on the front steps. We parted with a tearful goodbye on her part and a grateful hug on mine as Eric drove up in a dark green Mercedes sedan. I was glad he had left his Hummer at home; my game leg and cane made negotiating its doors difficult. We proceeded majestically through the nippy November air and still glorious foliage of the tree-lined drive up to the guesthouse. After the now familiar tumultuous greeting of the dogs, Eric helped me up the steps. This time I noticed a modest sign on the door identifying it as "The Nest." A man in work denims, probably in his 60s, brawny, and with graying hair and twinkling blue eyes, met us.

"This fellow is Jean-Paul DuPre, my right-hand man. He and his wife keep the place going. Anything doesn't work, or it's broke and needs repair, just press two on the house phone and J.P.'s your man."

J.P. put out his hand and said, "Welcome to The Nest, Ms. Bonham. I've turned on the heat. Eric can show you how to adjust the thermostat. Marianne fixed the coffee pot—just flip the switch—and put out sandwiches and fruit. She also stocked the cupboards and refrigerator with a few staples. You can also reach her any time by pressing two. I'll bring in your stuff. Which bedroom do you prefer?"

"The one by the deck, I think. Nice to meet you."

Eric picked up again, "If you need help unpacking, call Marianne. You look tired. I hope after a rest you can come over to the main house for dinner this evening. Nothing fancy so don't dress up. That green door over across the main drive is our everyday entry .We start to gather in around 5 P.M. What's the matter?"

I was overwhelmed by the consideration and care taken to make me welcome. To my great surprise, I found my eyes brimming with tears that spilled over my cheeks. Me, who had learned and resolved never to cry, wept. Eric was solicitous.

"There's Kleenex in the bathroom. Don't cry. Why are you crying?"

"I'm just so grateful for this welcome and this lovely place...."

Facing with an emotional female, he said with typical male embarrassment and diffidence, "Oh, well, that's all right, then. Have some lunch and a lie-down. We'll hope to see you this evening."

When he left I went to investigate the lunch laid out for me: two sandwiches, one ham and cheese, the other peanut butter and grape jelly; a bowl of apples, oranges, and a couple of bananas. Further investigation of refrigerator and cupboards disclosed cornflakes, instant oatmeal, an assortment of canned soups, peanut butter, and a loaf of bread; in the refrigerator milk and butter, lettuce, fresh mushrooms, green onions, and two kinds of salad dressing; in the freezer, a selection of frozen vegetables, a couple of one-pound packages of ground beef, and a half-gallon carton of butter pecan ice cream. The latter was a nice touch; the hospital served ice cream three meals out of five, but always vanilla. I never thought I would weary of vanilla ice cream but I couldn't wait to get at that butter pecan. I ate with appetite and poured a cup of coffee, then opened a panel of the bamboo blind and settled on a sofa in the living room.

The panorama and activity to be seen through the vast expanse of glass was a delight. Leaves, brown and gold, were beginning to drift down; in another week or so, bare branches would make a lacy screen across the view. Birds were quarreling and chaffering, fluttering and darting through the branches. An aggressive male cardinal slammed against the glass, a Canada jay jeered at his discomfiture. Two squirrels, their cheeks swollen with the harvest garnered from the huge oaks farther down the slope, scurried along their aerial highways. I resolved on my next trip to town, I would lay in my art supplies. Here was no dearth of subject matter for sketches and aquatints. Then lulled by the warmth and comfort, I fell sound asleep. I woke startled as the cardinal made another attack on his reflection. It was 3:30, time to get ready for my dinner engagement.

I hobbled across the drive to the green "everyday" door and was raising my hand to knock when it opened. Before me was six feet of lanky boy strongly resembling his father and accompanied by the elderly retriever. Auburn-haired, grey-eyed, the boy smiled broadly through the usual mass of dental hardware that seems to decorate every teenager's mouth. His bony face and frame held clear promise of husky and handsome maturity. The dog was wagging his hips and tail so hard he staggered as he pushed his nose into my free hand.

"I'm Don, Ms. Bonham. I was watching for you. Arthur! Bed!"

This to the dog who departed obediently to a pile of blankets in the far corner of the room. The boy continued, "Arthur is the only dog allowed in the house, Pancho and Cleo live in the barn. He's a sweet old fella but he likes to lean on people and that don't seem a good idea for you. Let me help you over this sill. This is our mud room. My responsibility is to keep clean and neat."

He made an expansive gesture to indicate a spotless tile floor and a row of winter coats hanging on one wall and outdoor footgear arranged neatly on the floor beneath. There seemed to be no better rejoinder than "And a good job, too." The boy bobbed his head to acknowledge the compliment and conducted me into the adjoining room. It was a room for living, a family's room, windows on both sides, an enormous fieldstone fireplace at the far end, a short wall of bookshelves, plump colorful leather sofas and chairs with lamps placed conveniently for reading and small glass-topped tables inviting books or bowls of snacks. Navaho rugs woven in earth tones lay scattered over the hardwood floor. The TV set was the least prominent piece of furniture in the room. "Mary's trimmings" were judiciously disposed here and there. I found myself unable to take my eyes off one piece that I was sure was her choice. It was an alabaster statue about 18 inches tall, two mythic figures, Hebe and Ganymede intertwined to raise a cup over their heads to Zeus, father of the Greek gods. I noticed that Don studiously avoided looking at it. He settled me on a sofa and headed off to the dining room.

"Make yourself comfortable, I got to get on the job; I set the table," he called back.

The next arrival was a stout black-haired, black-eyed woman, 50ish I guessed, dressed in a stylish denim shirtwaist dress. She held out a hand toward me, breathlessly announcing herself as Marianne. "Oh, Ms. Bonham, we're so happy to have you with us. Did you find everything over at The Nest? Now, remember, if you need anything, press two on the house phone. Either J.P. or I will answer. Would you like a drink before dinner?"

I told her that medication forced me to teetotal so she offered lemonade instead. I told her what I really wanted was for everyone to call me Thena or Athena; Ms. Bonham was too formal. She nodded smiling. When she regained control over her breathing, I decided she wasn't asthmatic, just hurried. I subsequently learned she lived a in a constant flurry and her panting was due to a tightly-laced corset supporting a bad back. She excused herself to put the finishing touches on dinner and hustled back to the kitchen. I was alone for a few minutes with time to look around and savor the ambience of the room. Every piece in it seemed to have been chosen for a family's comfort and an easy life style, although it didn't look like a page from *House and Garden*. The accessories were eclectic but so naturally disposed that they fitted with each other and everything else. Mary's hand, I surmised.

Then Eric blew in, freshly clean shaven, wearing casual clothes, and accepting the glass of wine Marianne offered. We three sat chatting until interrupted by Dora drifting elegantly into the scene, still garbed in her school uniform of pleated plaid kilt, knee socks, and button-down shirt, but with the added features of high heels, a floating feather boa, and elbow-length satin gloves.

"Ah, hello, dahlings," she caroled in an exaggerated British accent as she swung the ends of her boa in a wide arc. "How lovely the evening is. The cahlla lilies are in bloom and how happy we should be to be togethah. Welcome, welcome, Ms. Bonham."

She was beautiful as only a 16-year old girl in blooming health and joyous mood could be: dark auburn hair, sparkling green eyes, rose-petal complexion, a slender graceful body that even her outrageous outfit could not disguise. Eric made haste to explain.

"This is Dora. She has just captured the role of Blithe Spirit in her high school play and she punishes us with character development at every opportunity. Take off that stuff and come shake hands like a normal person. Then, haven't you got work to do?"

She laughed, obeyed, and excused herself. "My job is to put the food on the table. See ya there."

"Great kids," I commented, hoping I didn't sound patronizing. "They seem very attentive to their responsibilities."

"Yeah, with an occasional and forgivable lapse. Mary and I made them working partners in family operations from the time they could be trusted to carry a cup and saucer. Mary saw that as character-building discipline and frankly, she was right. Marianne and J.P. couldn't keep this big house clean and uncluttered if we didn't all pitch in. There's J.P. now, waving us in to dinner."

5

The table was set with coarse linen napery and brilliantly colored dishes decorated with Mexican motifs. Eric took his seat at the head of the table, dishing out slices from a huge ham and passing the plates to his right to Marianne who garnished them with mounds of sweet and Irish potato. Don added a hot roll to each plate and passed it to me to pass on. Shallow bowls of green salad stood at each place. I was stationed at the foot of the table with Don at my left and J.P. on my right. Dora at Eric's left started salad dressing around after the last meat serving. With full plates in front of us, silence fell seemingly by mutual consent while Marianne and J.P. said a brief grace and crossed themselves. Then chatter punctuated by the clink of utensils on plates broke out like a summer storm. When a report of Don's D in English put him under a cloud, Dora in a fit of sibling rivalry took pains to boast an A earned for her essay on apartheid. I noticed that Arthur had sneaked in under the table and was parked on Don's foot. J.P. announced the farrier was due to put the horses in shape for winter weather.

Marianne was engaged in telling Eric of her aggravation with a dilatory plumber but interrupted herself to ask me if I liked the menu and whether my servings were adequate. I told her after living for months under a tent in Borneo on SPAM and tinned peas, and then for weeks on bland hospital food, this dinner was food for the gods. Don leaped at a chance to hear more about Borneo and I favored him with a story of bower birds and their curious courting behaviors. He was rapt. Dora who was listening as avidly commented that there was a boy in her class who must have some bower bird DNA because he had a trinket every day for the next girl he wanted to date. From that she turned to her dad; the school's harvest dance was imminent and she absolutely had nothing to wear. Lamenting that her clothing allowance was all used up, she was trying to negotiate funds for a new dress. Don said she could have his clothes allowance, he had a lot left and didn't take much stock in clothes. Marianne brought him up short with a reminder.

"Not so fast, you're due for a new dress suit; your arms and legs are hanging out by inches from the cuffs of your old one."

The currents of conversation volleyed and swirled across the table, good-natured, generally polite, one topic tripping on the heels of another, adult and teen topics intermixed. It occurred to me that this was how a successful family interacted, enmeshed in the triumphs and failures, concerns and joys, of each and all. It was new to me and I found it wonderfully warm and thoroughly admirable. I knew nostalgia for an world I had never experienced except vicariously in old movies. The conversation began to focus on Don's shortcomings in English as he bemoaned an assignment to write a report on birds.

"I got a book but the ones I see don't look like their pictures, and if I blow this report, I'll have another D," he grumbled.

I was bold enough to volunteer help. "You know, I'm a biologist and a certified teacher and have had experience in writing and editing. Perhaps I could help you with your project; I'd be happy to."

Don's face grew bright with interest. "Could we do it on the bower birds? They're cool. If it's OK with Dad, I wish you would."

When I looked at Eric, I noticed a glimmer of worry in his eyes vanishing behind a dawning glint of optimism. Clearly, the boy hadn't been handling his mother's death well and Eric was grateful for his reaction.

"It's not up to me. If Thena can spare the time, I won't complain."

"I'll be available every afternoon. I'll be gone to rehab sessions in the morning, providing they ever deliver my car."

Dora blushed and hastened to apologize,

"I took a call from the dealer just before I came to dinner. He said expect delivery around ten tomorrow morning, and he hoped you could drive him back to the store. I got so excited to meet you, I forgot. I'm sorry. Now I better bring in dessert. It's our favorite, fresh pineapple with coconut milk dressing."

We repaired to the family room with our coffee while the children cleared the table and loaded the dishwasher. Arthur followed us as unobtrusively as a big dog could and heaved himself down on the hearth with a gusty sigh. He gave the impression that his presence in the living room was just barely tolerated. A burst of song from the *Mikado* in a clear alto and a fragile tenor, interspersed with squawks and whistles (I assumed the cockatoo's contribution) came from the kitchen. Shortly thereafter, a line of four cats strolled in from the dining room and Eric called out in exasperation.

"Dora, didn't I tell you to keep those cats in your room? Thena may not like cats or she may be allergic. I'm sorry, Thena. You already know Don is Dogmaster—well, Dora is Catmistress. She's currently under orders to eliminate the last of an unforeseen batch of kittens. She loses no opportunity to parade them in hope of pawning off that black one on one of our guests."

"I like cats, although I've never owned or been owned by one. Do they have names?"

Dora must have been waiting for a reaction; she immediately popped up to introduce her charges—the orange tabby, Prince Peter; the part-Siamese, Mrs. Anna; the gray and black tiger, Angelina, and her barely-weaned offspring Zorro, a black male with blazing green eyes. I suspected an ulterior motive when Dora picked up Zorro and deposited him in my lap. He sat docile and staring but making no effort to be ingratiating, even when I caressed him.

"He's been hard to place because he's not very outgoing. Don't you think he would make a good companion for you over in The Nest?"

"Now, Dora!" Eric protested.

"I don't know much about looking after a cat, Dora. Do you think I'd make a good companion for him?"

"Oh, yes." Enthusiasm bubbled over in her voice. "I can bring over a litter box and a bag of litter and a bag of dry food, and food and water dishes. He wouldn't be any trouble at all. I'll even come and clean the litter box. What do you say?"

"You're making me an offer I can hardly refuse. Especially about the litter box. Can't he go outside? The cats I've known before didn't need a litter box."

Dora explained about an aggressive male raccoon who had already killed one kitten that had escaped by an open door. And about the occasional coyote that prowled the area. And about the Cooper's hawk that often soared over the field looking for prey. She made it very clear to me that Zorro had to be a house cat. She furnished me with a book on cat care and promised to keep me posted on the schedule of vet visits and treatments. Eric was watching with a quizzical look on his face.

"Maybe Thena will think Zorro is more of a responsibility than she wants. She might not have time or energy …."

"Yes, I will," I interrupted. "Thinking about an animal companion will be good for me, distract me from my aches and pains. And I'll have Dora to back me up if need be."

And so, the die was cast. The next morning before Dora left for school she outfitted me with cat and gear and Zorro took up residence at The Nest.

6

My new car was delivered as promised at 10 A.M. After I drove the dealer's man back to the shop, I stopped at an art supply store and stocked up on the wherewithal for my projected art work. Zorro greeted me at the door upon my return, unrepentant for the ravages he had visited on the toilet paper roll. He watched with great interest as I picked up shreds and wads of paper from the floor. I resolved to keep the bathroom door closed henceforth. I phoned the rehab clinic and made the arrangements for daily visits. I also made up my shopping list for a stop at the grocery. Lunch out of the way, I set up an easel before the big window and achieved a single charcoal sketch before I tired out. I woke from a nap on the sofa with a black face full of green eyes staring point blank into my face. Zorro was perched on my chest, the deep rumble of a purr starting in his chest. I had been elected a location satisfactory for cat napping.

Don and Arthur came knocking around four o'clock. I invited them in and suggested hereafter entry with just a knock and a yoohoo would save me a few steps. Don was carrying his laptop and a wad of printouts. Arthur greeted Zorro with a wet but friendly caress and the two of them settled down comfortably on the hearth.

"I got a whole bunch of stuff off the Net," Don said, triumphantly waving his papers.

I complimented him on his industry and but drew a blank stare when I asked him how he planned to deal with his subject. The idea of an outline seemed completely foreign to him. After a lot of questions and answers, he had worked out a three-part attack: local wild birds; pet birds; exotic birds. Did he have a title for his report? More questions and answers and the title emerged as "Behavior of Birds." All birds, or selected species? By this time he was scratching his head in frustration.

"When do I get to write something? This don't seem to be getting my report down, does it?"

"Have you heard the carpenter's maxim? Measure twice, cut once! Now then, you've been measuring; you've decided on a focus—behavior—for your report and selected targets—types of birds—for commentary. Now you can narrow your approach to certain birds from those types. What are your ideas?"

"I'll use the cardinal and the jay and maybe a hawk for examples of wild bird behavior, our cockatoo Oscar for a pet bird, bower birds and another one I found—a caracara—for the exotic ones. I can say what I observe about the first two kinds, and what I read about the exotic ones. Satisfied?"

He was grinning and grinned even more broadly when I said,

"There now, it seems to me your report is almost done. Just add the words."

His face fell. "That's where I lose the most points—on spelling and grammar and something Teach calls syntax." I suggested that tonight he write the sentences to fill out his outline and tomorrow we would tackle trouble spots. He was enthusiastic about his project but when I shifted uneasily in my chair (I was getting tired), he became solicitous.

"Gee, I'm sorry. Did working on my report make you hurt?"

"No, I always hurt, sometimes worse and sometimes less. I just a little tired."

His face grew dark and distorted with remembered grief and he blurted out,

"My mom never admitted she hurt. She lied to me when I asked. Said not to worry, it didn't amount to anything."

I sensed the anger over his mother's death festering inside of him. She had left him behind, bypassed and cheated, resentful that she had not shared her suffering with him. Maybe he felt had she spoken of her pain, he could have helped her to bear it. The sense of responsibility she had fostered in him as he grew had become a kind of curse. I decided to open my heart to him.

"Well, a person like me living with constant physical pain doesn't like to talk about it a lot. My leg often hurts so badly I think I can't stand it. I don't exactly lie when someone asks about it. I answer but I just don't tell all of my feelings; I think of it as consideration for other people's feelings. I don't see any reason to make anyone else miserable with my misery. I'm grateful that they care but I can't expect they can do anything about it. Maybe your mom loved you too much to burden you with her trouble. Moms are like that."

What a hypocrite I was! Pontificating about the selflessness of mothers when.... But, oddly Don appeared to take my sanctimony in good part. He gulped down some unshed tears, nodded, and packed up his stuff. Just then the cardinal launched an attack on the window. The crash and flutter startled Zorro and Arthur out of their doze and gave Don a welcome change of topic.

"Why does he do that? Don't it smart?"

"When you read up on *Cardinalis cardinalis*, you'll discover the males are fiercely territorial and our friend there thinks the reflection he sees in the window is another male encroaching on his territory. That's a behavior worth noting in your report, isn't it?"

"Hey, yeah, cool. See ya tomorrow. OK?"

I wondered as I watched him and Arthur leave whether our talk about moms would bear fruit.

7

The days began to pass, pleasantly for the most part. The Nest was proving to be an ideal place to convalesce and begin a career in illustrative arts. Those vast windows looked out on a fascinating world. Immediately under the windows lay a neglected terrace supported by a freestone wall, where ground squirrels and a four-foot blacksnake lived in ivied crevices and on sunny days basked or frisked on the coping stones. From time to time a fox prowled the terrace to prey on a flourishing population of voles. His luck with ground squirrels wasn't very good. From a row of dwarf yews just outside the stone wall a brushy slope fell away for some hundred yards toward five enormous old oak trees strung out at its foot. The yews and random evergreen trees made a green contrast to the fall foliage of orange and yellow leaves. When snow fell during December and January, the winter landscape was punctuated by the red glitter of sumac. Springtime brought thickets of dogwood and wild plum bursting into bloom and trilliums, Solomon's seal, and violets emerging from the deep leaf mold beneath the canopy. When I sang my praises of the slope and its flora and fauna, J.P. looked sheepish and apologized for letting it go to rack and ruin. In the old days, he said, he had kept the brush controlled and flower beds weeded. He brightened when I begged him to leave it untouched and said cultivation would spoil its charm.

The ground and trees were alive with wildlife. Until he (or she) hibernated, a possum frequented the scene, rooting around in the drifts of fallen leaves. A female skunk and her three kits trotted along at first in a neat file, then as the kits matured, the family scattered on individual projects. An occasional encounter with a dog or coyote led to an odorous reminder of their unseen presence; otherwise I followed their paths by the erect plumes of their tails moving through the tall grass. A fat groundhog toddled around in fair weather. The bird count was large and varied: cardinals, jays, buntings, house wrens, goldfinches, robins, a wood duck nesting in a hollow stump. An owl picked off two ducklings as they followed their mother one evening to the brook in the valley meadow. There was no lack of inspiration for my brush and charcoal pencil, and I reveled in my opportunities.

Visits to the clinic seemed to be helping my leg and when I dropped in for a quick visit with Lita she commented enthusiastically on the improvement. Nevertheless I was still obliged to use an electric cart to shop the supermarket and to be judicious in managing the bags from car to house. Don brought home an A and a "Much improved" in red ink on his bird report. I was invited to dinner at the main house a couple of times a week, once for Dora to show off her hard-won party dress. Don and Dora dropped in daily for utilitarian or social visits; Eric often stopped by in the evening for coffee and chat. After another of Don's literary triumphs, Eric voiced his pleasure and gratitude for my work with the boy.

"He's doing well in school, not just in English. It's as if he has developed some peace of mind and can concentrate on his schoolwork. I think he values your tutelage and friendship. He's not becoming a nuisance, is he?"

"Not at all," I hastened to reassure him. "He's a good kid and I enjoy him. I enjoy Dora too. She was so beautiful in her pink gown, I hope you took pictures."

"I didn't care for the low cut of that bodice but when both Marianne and you approved, I decided not to be a fuddy-duddy. The kids think very well of you. I'm glad you came to The Nest. Are you happy here?"

"Very. I'll be very sorry to move on. The Harald family is more of a family than I have ever had in my life."

"Cats, dogs, and all, eh? Incidentally, that sketch of Zorro is very good. Are you finding purchasers for your pieces?"

I told him the art supply shop had a display area and several of my items had sold promptly and profitably. As conversation languished and we ran out of trivia, Eric began to squirm a bit in his chair. Finally, he turned his discomfort into words.

"Say, are you feeling well enough these days to go out to dinner and a movie? I'll take the Mercedes if you need special incentive."

I laughed and told him to say when. He replied with a question, "Tomorrow, about six?" and I agreed in a hurry. A few minutes after he had left, I found myself doing some arithmetic. Marianne had told me of plans she had for celebrating his 40th birthday on January 4th. I had just passed my 30th. Was I willing to ignore a 10-year difference in age? But as I juggled my cane and the tray of cups and saucers on the way to the kitchen, I chided myself. Why should I sweat an age difference? A leg forever maimed was more of a wet blanket for notions of romance. The fling I had had with one of the editors at EcoProductions was troubled enough when I was whole; I wasn't sure I was capable of a relationship now that I was "handicapped." There I had used the hateful word! I drew a deep breath and went off to bed. Zorro was waiting in a furry black ball at the foot; his purr swelled in diapason as I slid under the covers.

Eric had made reservations at *Le Paon*, a restaurant so upscale that its menu was done in calligraphy on parchment. In the dim lighting the rich flourishes reduced the dishes to illegibility, ditto the wine list. I took a coward's way out and asked Eric to order for me.

"OK," he said, "I can do that. I'm something of a regular here. It's a great place to entertain clients especially when they bring their wives along. One of them, Mrs. Who-sis, raves about the 'cachet' and always orders the least appropriate and most expensive wine on the list. I take it you are still on the wagon. How about beef? Rare, well, or in between?"

A medium-well *filet mignon* sauced with perfect Bearnaise, presented with perfectly cooked asparagus, carrots, and cauliflower was just right. Crusty French bread with garlicky olive oil for dipping made a perfect side. The perfect dessert was *crème brûlée* and the coffee was

Colombian. I sat back in my chair, replete and sighing in satisfaction. Eric laughed.

"I didn't know you were such a trencherwoman," he said. "You always seem to enjoy our homely meals but tonight you outdid your reputation. Pardon me for descending to personalities. I'm hoping your appetite is an indicator of your improving health."

"It's a combination of ambience and intimacy," I admitted unblushingly. "I love the delicious food and lively talk of Harald family dinners. Nevertheless, it's especially nice to have only one person to speak and listen to. The hubbub of give and take sometimes drags me under. Please understand, I'm not complaining. Its just that I find this a very pleasant experience."

"We'll have to do it often then. Are we ready to go now?"

When I said yes and started to rise, he told me to stay for a moment. His face grew very serious and he reached across the table to take my hand.

"This has been a fantastic evening for me. I haven't enjoyed a woman's company so much since I lost Mary. I hope you will let me spend more time with you, time like this. I find your company delightful both at home and in public and I have grown more than fond of you. I want…"

I interrupted. I had been expecting some kind of an understated pass before the evening concluded and took immediate steps to defuse what I feared might become a serious situation.

"Eric," I answered, "I like you very much and I enjoy spending time with you, but I think you should put aside any romantic notions you may harbor. I have only now accepted the fact that I'm a cripple" [I almost choked on the word] "and this damn lingering infection threatens my overall health. I can barely walk 100 yards and I'm swallowing pills by the handfuls just to keep my fever at bay and my pain tolerable. I refuse to whine or complain but the truth is, I'm not fit to be the object of anyone's fervent affection."

His face mirrored his disappointment. I was sure he had planned to continue with an even warmer expression of regard, but he accepted my rebuff, bottled up his emotion, and said lightly,

"OK, I'll back off. But I won't change my mind." He drew a deep sigh and made an effort to change the subject. "Sorry to say, I didn't get tickets for anything but it's still early enough for a movie, provided you aren't too tired. What do you say? The Cinema Center is playing *Fantasia* or the Rialto has *On Golden Pond* and The Rave has *Master and Commander*. Not a very sophisticated bill of fare but each of them is a prize winner."

I opted for *Fantasia;* it had been a bright spot in my loveless childhood and I had heard it was newly restored. I prattled happily about how much I loved the dancing hippos and Mickey as *The Sorcerer's Apprentice.* The rest of the evening passed pleasantly despite some awkwardness in our conversation.

The awkwardness gradually dissipated as we fell back into our routine of our casual evenings, but Eric's disclosure of interest lingered in the back of both our minds. My discomfort stemmed from a concern that he was probably motivated less by romantic attraction than by my suitability to replace Mary as mother to his children. But I put my notions firmly aside and concentrated on getting on with my recovery—such as it promised to be. Weekday mornings devoted to rehab massage and hydrotherapy dwindled from five times a week to three, I worked on sketches and pastels in the afternoons, the children ran in and out before and after school, Eric dropped in for coffee two or three evenings a week—I was becoming too busy to dwell on my disability. The long, dark hours of the night remained difficult but Zorro's furry bulk draped across my knees or ankles was both distracting and soothing.

Practice had restored my old facility with art materials and Lord knows I had plenty of subjects in the Harald menagerie and the wildlife outside my windows. I decided to gift the family with framed sketches for Christmas. The outcome was a set of pieces: a pastel of Dora's three cats as a multi-colored ball asleep in a basket, a charcoal sketch of Arthur in a noble pose, and an aquatint of Oscar with his crest fully deployed. The set was received with delight and warm praise at the Christmas gift exchange but the family's one-upmanship rather floored me. They had pooled their resources to give me a combination TV and DVD player. When I protested, Eric said,

"If you don't want to accept it as a personal gift, look at it as an addition to the furnishing of The Nest. We're over there so much, your living room is just an extension of this one. Besides, I find looking at movies with you in the evening is very relaxing. "

In the end I stopped protesting. But I didn't stop sketching and painting the Harald animals. In April, Dora introduced me to Torold the tortoise, recently out of hibernation and now roaming the flower bed next to the main house. Torold took his name from Eric's grandfather and had been thoroughly tamed by the children.

"Chirp like a cricket," Dora instructed me, "and he'll come for a treat. He likes grapes and crisp lettuce. I suppose it makes a nice change from worms and insects he gathers on his own."

Tyra Swann, at the art store in town, was growing more and more excited by my output. She begged the loan of my portfolio to take with her to Chicago and show to friends there. She returned towing C. William Pattison, a publisher of children's books. He was boiling over with enthusiasm to do a book illustrated with sketches of Oscar, Torold, and Zorro. C. William, Bill for short, had assigned a staff writer to making a story board, and upon reviewing the outline, I had to admit the project sounded feasible. Soon, I had added it to my activities.

8

The story created an unlikely *ménage à trois* in which Zorro, Oscar, and Torold, bored with a humdrum home life, ventured out to experience a series of hairbreadth escapes. I was given the opportunity to depict a disheveled Oscar rescued from a violent storm of wind and rain, an unhappy Zorro isolated on the tiptop branch of a tree and threatened by a hawk, a philosophical Torold observing and offering advice and comfort from ground level. It was fun and by May I had assembled a collection of drawings for the writer to weave into text. The project had called for frequent visits from Bill Pattison, rather to Eric's ill-concealed annoyance. I suspected he viewed Bill as a rival. I know the children did. Bill was about my age, tall and lanky, with a sort of rough-hewn face and an unruly mop of hair. He dressed himself at Brooks Brothers and drove a sleek silver Jag. Don envied him the car but Dora dismissed him as a pretentious middle-aged (about my age!) Ivy Leaguer without redeeming attributes. Sensitive to the aura of disapproval hovering over contacts with the Haralds, Bill usually met me at Tyra's shop or took me to dinner in order to discuss the project.

I had negotiated with Eric for an extension of my residence at The Nest. He was more than willing for me to stay on. Don had completed the winter quarter with an impressive array of A's and B's. Although my attentions had helped, his success was really due to a new ability to apply himself. Despite Dora's conviction that thirty was the threshold of senility, she decided to overlook my advanced age and make me a confidante. We regularly hashed over he-said, she-said stories of boy-girl dilemmas, although mostly I listened. Dora's attitude toward romantic connections was still nascent, more of the order of observation than participation. By June my limp had improved considerably and I walked cane in hand, rather than lurched, to my seat at the honors convocation at Dora's and Don's school. The cane and an unobtrusive cloth brace continued to be necessary to stabilize that left leg but the pain had subsided to a dull ache most of the time. In May I ventured on short daily walks on level ground around the buildings. Routinely accompanied by the canine trio, I made equine acquaintances with carrots across the paddock fence and observed new additions to the Harald menagerie—peacocks!

The peacocks were a gift to Eric from a friend whose suburban neighbors had vigorously complained at the eldritch screeches that rang out day and night over his neighborhood. They arrived named Him and Her but the children promptly rechristened them Buster and Bertha. They took to the Harald property with zest, perching on the rooftrees of the barn and sheds and rummaging for worms and bugs in the loose detritus under the trees. That put them frequently in view from my windows and I was getting ideas for a second book where Buster and Bertha joined Zorro, Oscar, and Torold in further adventures. Don had worried originally about attacks by predators but after witnessing Buster's triumphant encounter with an unwary coyote, he stopped worrying. "Old Buster can take care of himself," he reported. "He's a better watchdog than Pancho or Cleo ever pretended to be."

By August the OZT (shorthand for the adventures of Oscar, Zorro, and Torold) book was in the bookstores and going like hot cakes. Bill was after me for a sequel to include Buster. His writer had created another story board to challenge my artistic abilities. With the royalties rolling in, my financial situation appeared optimistic. Bill's writer had assumed the marketing chores and much to my relief, I was spared bookstore appearances and signings. Buster was scheduled to make his debut with OZT in time for the Christmas trade. I was astounded as well as pleased with the rapidity with which Bill's publishing house produced and promoted the books. I had settled into life on the Harald spread so contentedly that the thought of moving on rarely crossed my mind.

Throughout the spring, Dora had been working on a driver's license. With a learner's permit and a licensed driver as passenger, she had been allowed to take the farm car, a battered Ford Escort that J.P. had put in perfect mechanical condition, out in traffic. I was often asked to be the obligatory passenger and her frequent trips to get driving experience facilitated my grocery shopping and visits to Tyra Swann's shop. Don's nose was somewhat out of joint as Dora's project cut into my time, especially since he suspected Eric intended to spoil her with a car of her own. Eric did buy a used VW bug, undented and bright yellow, but made her responsible for gas, maintenance, and insurance. Looking for a job to pay off his startup loan, she jumped on Tyra's offer of two hours in the shop daily after school and on Saturday mornings. Don soon saw the advantage of riding to school with Dora. Freed from the morning school bus schedule, he gained an extra hour of sleep. He enjoyed his advantage only in May, school was out on June 1.

The first event of summer business was for Don and Dora to take the cats and dogs to the vet for their annual checkups and immunizations. Zorro was required to stay for two days to be neutered and to have his front paws declawed. He returned grumpy and disheveled and spent the next two days hiding under my bed, licking his wounds and grooming himself. He emerged favoring his front feet; I could empathize with his limp although I envied its transience. Don and Dora both went to camp that summer, he to the Boy Scout Jamboree in August, she to Bell's Equitation Ranch for two weeks in July. I don't know who in the Harald family missed them most. I only know I missed them a lot. The frequency of Eric's evening visits for coffee and a movie increased.

9

A week after school started in the fall, the afternoon of September 12th to be exact, I was napping when thunderous knocking erupted at the door of The Nest. Waking startled from a deep sleep set my heart racing and stomach churning. I struggled to my feet and to the door where a postal employee with a clipboard required me to identify myself and to sign for a registered letter. Puzzled to receive registered mail, I read the return address on the envelope: Woodbridge Hall, Troy Junction, New York. Memory triggered a sense of foreboding as I recognized the name of the facility where my mother had been confined for the past twenty some years. I hobbled to sit down at the kitchen table and then slowly and reluctantly worried the envelope open with shaking hands; I spread the enclosed letter flat to read it. Zorro who had run for cover in fear of the unwonted racket now cautiously emerged from under a bed and came to rub against my ankles. Grateful for the distraction I reached down to caress his smooth black fur. I was loath to read the letter. I felt that the longer I could put off learning the contents, the longer I could retain my peace of mind. Then, drawing a long breath, I knew I could not delay longer. Good news, bad news, or no news, I was obliged to deal with it.

The words that leaped off the page were "the death of Alicia Bonham. Our records name you as next of kin, and we are contacting you for instruction as to disposition of her remains." In my shock

35

and dismay I was thinking why, if the State of New York had been responsible for my mother for twenty years, did it now make me responsible for "disposition of her remains." Crazy questions ran across my mind. Wasn't possession nine tenths of the law? Hadn't 20 years of New York's possession of Alicia Bonham's living body entitled it to her dead body? For a moment I cursed my name listed as next of kin on a piece of paper in some dusty file. Fleetingly I wondered how the officials at the institution had found my current address. But, of course, Uncle George. I had cited him as a reference when I applied for the job at Nature Productions and I had kept that snippy Director of Human Resources informed in case working there ever became possible. Resentment briefly flared; I valued anonymity. Then, a degree of reason returning, I had to acknowledge that Uncle George had been freed of the responsibility for my mother as soon as the State of New York had taken charge. He had every right to identify me as adult next of kin and to indicate there was no one else to be notified or to take ownership of her remains. The letter expressed sympathy and condolences in canned phrases and listed a telephone number, available from 8 A.M. to 5 P.M. Eastern Standard Time, Monday through Friday. Bruno Zloty, Deputy Administrator, requested a reply as soon as possible.

I sat there, absentmindedly stroking Zorro who had now established himself in my lap as I read and reread the three paragraphs of Bruno Zloty's letter. What to do next? Eric was away on business. If he were home, I might confide in him. Might! But maybe not! I had kept my mother's existence a secret for more than twenty years. Except for a brief foray into the archives of the New York State legal system I had not pursued any word of her. Uncle George had told me years ago that she lived in a fog of the sedative drugs administered to make her controllable, her memory of me and her previous life gone, not happy, not unhappy, uncaring for more than meals and sleep. Whatever I would do, I would do on my own, for now keeping my secret mine alone. Deciding to call Woodbridge Hall in the morning and feeling like a consummate coward, I refolded the letter and put it in the pocket of my sweater.

Don and Arthur came bounding in at their usual time, Don bubbling over with enthusiasm for the challenges of the new school year, Arthur greeting Zorro with a lolloping tongue across the face.

Don's chief enthusiasms were algebra and the outstanding physical qualities of the new math teacher (female and young), followed by his acceptance to the soccer team, and the biology department's acquisition of an iguana. I listened with less than complete attention, as if the unwelcome racket of a jackhammer were pounding away while I was trying to listen to *Nova* on TV. Don soon tumbled to my distraction.

"Are you OK? Is this a bad day? I saw you taking a walk around the pond yesterday. I'll bet you overdid it."

I had to tell the boy something so I reassured him that my walk had had no bad effects. I said that news of the death of a distant relative might call me away for a day or so. The boy expressed condolences far more sincere than Bruno Zloty's.

"It's too bad Dad's away from home. He called last night from the Upper Peninsula and said he was going on to Northern Ontario and would be out of touch for three or four days. Something about atmospheric interference with satellite transmissions." Don proudly repeated the technical details he had obviously practiced to achieve exact relay. "If you need to go to the airport, J.P. can take you any time. Or Dora can take you when she gets off work. Just call us."

I thanked him and he departed whistling cheerily, Arthur limping behind him. I set myself to preparing my evening meal, my thoughts still in turmoil. My tomato soup burned on the bottom of the pan and I cut my finger slicing up a cucumber. I gave up early and retired to the bedroom like a surly old bear off to hibernation. Zorro followed, baffled at the omission of evening treats, but resigned with good grace to curl up at my feet. I didn't sleep well; I tried over and over to remember my mother's face but all I could conjure up was an image of a figure in a black coat hunched up on the back seat of the car that took her away from Aunt Julie's house. Then in memory I heard the cadences of her soft voice singing,

"Jesus loves me this I know, for the Bible tells me so,
Little ones to Him belong, I am weak but he is strong."
I finally fell asleep whispering those words into the darkness.

10

The next morning I charged Dora to look after Zorro in my absence. Then, I put a three-day supply of clothes into a back pack, tucked a stock of pain pills into my purse, renewed the rubber tip on my cane, and called Woodbridge Hall. Mr. Zloty gave me directions to Troy Junction on the assumption that I would rent a car and drive from the Albany airport. A long conversation with the airline got reservations for the itinerary to and from Albany. Asking no questions, offering no comment, wearing a worried look, J.P. drove me to the airport and promised to hand over the letter I was leaving for Eric as soon as Eric returned. The trip to Albany called for stops at three airports on the way and a lot of walking from gate to gate on the unyielding terrazzo of the concourses. My disabled status did not diminish the aggravations of security checks, had in fact increased them. The steel pins in my leg set off every metal detector I encountered and I was ushered repeatedly off to a side room for X-rays. Driving from Albany to the village of Troy Junction in a rented car was uneventful. I nevertheless arrived at my destination exhausted and aching, fetching up late in the afternoon at a pleasant little motel with a country kitchen restaurant where I spent an comfortable night and enjoyed a tasty breakfast. The desk clerk, a Bengali speaking meticulous English, directed me courteously to Woodbridge Hall, not without a curious look.

I arrived at the pillared gates of what looked like a luxurious estate until the car topped a slight rise and the building came into view. It was essentially a windowless monolith of cut stone, granite trim on limestone, with an imposing entrance on a curving drive where a bored but smartly uniformed guard occupied a sentry box. After displaying ID and Bruno Zloty's letter, I was allowed through a glass door, only to be hung up at another metal detector and searched by a large muscular female before being released to Mr. Zloty's office. I sat there waiting until a young woman in civilian clothes breezed in. She was obviously a devotee to the current fashions of female celebs with long corkscrew curls straggling down in front of their ears and breasts struggling to escape from the inadequate constraints of cotton knit and Spandex. Chewing gum with energy and panache, she informed me that Mr. Zloty was taking a few days off to fish. She reeked of so much cheap perfume and blatant sexuality that I could understand his effort to escape to fresh outdoor air. But then in my second thoughts, perhaps what he had was what he wanted. There's no accounting for tastes.

The badge teetering over her right bosom bore the name Shanda Vanderhoevel. Shanda started to push papers in front of me for signatures, explaining each as presented. "This here's a copy of the death certificate issued by the doctor here at the Hall. This here is the authorization to release the documents and belongings of the deceased to the next of kin, which is you, I guess. Sign it and keep the carbon. I need to see your ID. This is a map to the Watson Mortuary in Troy Junction; that's where the body is. And this," pushing a cheap fiberboard suitcase toward me with disdainful fingers, "is her belongings. There's an inventory inside."

"Is there anyone here who knew her?" I asked.

Shanda suspended mastication long enough to gape wide-eyed at me.

"Why? I never heard she left any words, never even talked. What can anybody tell you more than that?" she asked.

I insisted and finally Shanda said, "Well, there's Matron. I'll call her. Maybe she'll agree to talk to you."

Matron proved to be a large woman in rimless eyeglasses, a spotless starched white uniform, and a badge identifying her as Mrs. Maria

Gillis. Her first act was to hand me a printed form with **STATE OF NEW YORK** blazoned across the top.

"Fill this out with your complaints and mail it to the address indicated," she ordered.

"I haven't any complaints," I hastened to say. "I only wanted to know how Alicia Bonham died, whether she said anything, whether anyone was with her."

Matron favored me with a piercing look and apparently decided it was safe to confide in me.

"She died in her sleep. As far as anyone knows she hadn't spoken for fifteen years, ever since we started Thorazine. Until then, whatever she said was gibberish and she was violent and uncooperative. The medication made her docile but she slipped into catatonia, had to be dressed, fed, pottied, and so on."

"What did she die of?" I ventured to ask.

"There, on the death certificate. Heart failure." Then, taking pity on me, she elaborated, "She had developed right-sided heart failure and although we treated for it, it progressed. Is that all?"

Yes, I said, and left the office for the stark cleanliness of the halls and foyer. I'm sure the indoor temperature was a reasonable 70ish degrees but I emerged chilled to the bone. The building seemed uninhabited; the barren halls stretched away from the foyer, empty of human occupation. The polished linoleum floors echoed under my lonely footsteps. I might as well have been passing through the chambers of a tomb. I wondered what it was like behind the scenes where my mother had been housed and fed. I wondered if the sun shone there, if there were green grass or flowers to be seen, if the attendants ever spoke kindly to the inmates, if the food was properly cooked and dispensed, whether there were bars…. I had to stop wondering before tears blurred my eyes too much for driving. My emotions surprised me. Years of total rejection of all thoughts and concern for the woman who had given birth to me, 22 years after seeing the last of her, why now was I engulfed in sadness? I was willing to admit blood was thicker than water but I couldn't forget it was blood, the blood of innocents, that stood between us.

I found the Watson Mortuary without difficulty and presented my ID and the official papers from Woodbridge Hall. The undertaker was a smooth young fellow neatly dressed at this morning hour in a button-down shirt, pressed chinos, and penny moccasins. He showed me to a handsome office; his expression was blandly polite but his manner was businesslike and he dealt with our business efficiently. I squirmed while he informed me of every conceivable manner and level of funerary rites, illustrating his spiel with brochures and a photo album. Noting my restlessness, he put the brochures aside.

"We offer every service. We have a very fine line of caskets, with an excellent variety of linings. In this book we display a selection of floral blankets. I can arrange services for any denomination you designate; you have only to specify time and place, number expected to attend..." and on and on, right down to a grave marker. I opted for cremation, burial of the cremains in a four by four plot in a special area of the town cemetery, and a flat stone slab carved simply with "Alicia Ardith Bonham, 1960-2006."

"Where can I find a priest?" I asked.

I recalled that Aunt Julie was Catholic and perhaps my mother was also. But Mr. Watson said, "If you're not sure, I suggest you talk to the Unitarian minister. Father Sebastian is a stickler for the rules of Catholic interment and wouldn't take kindly to 'maybe' Catholic. He's been known to make an issue of residents of the Hall dying without last rites. The Reverend Mrs. Andrews is likely to be more accommodating, and she's a lovely woman besides."

Mr. Watson provided me with notarized copies of the death certificate and an application form for the Social Security death benefit, $250 against a total bill of $4,000! Before accepting my credit card in payment of his charges, he telephoned my bank. Wearily, I listened to his conversation and was grateful for the large balance remaining from the settlement of my injury. At last, straightening the stack of papers on his desk, he asked,

"Would you care to view the deceased now?"

I swallowed hard and nodded. He led me to a back hall and a window hung with a heavy drape. Positioning me in front of it, he rapped on the glass and an attendant inside drew the drape away, disclosing the frail husk of Alicia Ardith Bonham stretched on a gurney, a sheet drawn up to her chin. I drew a sharp breath. I saw her face, thinner but as unlined as my own, the same bone structure, and a mass of gray hair that once must have been the same bronzy gold as mine.

A faint tracery of fine blue veins lay on her closed eyelids. A trick of the embalmer's art had contrived a faint smile on the delicate curve of the ashen lips. For a moment my head swam and I had to shuffle my feet to stay upright. I felt Mr. Watson's hand under my elbow but I shook it off, turned, and walked back along the hall to the office where, my knees gone rubbery, I sat down. Mr. Watson followed and stood helplessly by while I gathered my composure. Then I bade him good-bye and thank-you and left to find The Reverend Ms. Andrews.

The Reverend's church was just three doors down the street. I entered tentatively, worried by the clatter I created in closing the door. Reverend Andrews was an elderly woman, stocky, ruddy-faced, and carefully coiffed. Dressed in jeans, a sweat shirt and clerical collar, she was cleaning the sanctuary in an aura of Murphy's Oil Soap. She laid aside her rag and bucket to hear my requests, and then agreed to hold a brief committal service when Watson's was ready to turn over Alicia Bonham's ashes. If she thought my lack of emotion and decision not to stay for the ceremony strange, she didn't say anything. She did ask me to sit down in a pew while she recited the Lord's Prayer and the Twenty-third Psalm. Softly and sincerely inflected, her voice lent genuine meaning to the familiar phrases. As she finished, she smiled brightly and said,

"There, those words are for you. I'll select equally reassuring passages for Alicia Bonham's service. Go in peace and the love of God."

I stumbled out into the daylight and back to the car feeling as hollow as an empty bucket—all of it over and done. What more was there, I wondered. Well, I found out—dozing on the plane homeward bound, dreaming snatches of nightmare, waking in a panic, hoping I was concealing my distress from my seatmate. Mentally reviewing the paper work I had accumulated at Woodbridge Hall and Watson's Mortuary merely added to the stress. I had emptied Alicia's fiberboard suitcase before I left my motel room and started back to Albany. The meager contents included a neat black dress with a white Peter Pan collar, a lightweight black jacket, a set of underwear pretty but unworn, a handful of toilet articles (comb, brush, nail file, nothing showing signs of use), a small tin box of trinkets, and a slim packet of letters tied with a pink ribbon. I put the box of trinkets and the letters in my backpack, along with the file folder and bundled papers from Woodbridge Hall and the mortuary. The rest of the stuff stayed in the motel room when I departed. Leaving Troy Junction and driving to Albany was simple enough. The demands of traffic kept my concentration engaged and only fleeting thoughts of Alicia Ardith Bonham crossed my mind. But once in flight, the adrenaline pump shut down and Alicia's face, all the signatures I had put on papers, and a disorganized myriad of unhappy thoughts started to dance in my inward gaze. In the meantime, my left leg was reacting to the unwonted punishment of excessive walking on hard surfaces by ballooning with edema. I hobbled down the stairs from the plane at Avalon Airport, half-dazed and wholly worn out. Entering the airport lobby, I walked into Eric's arms, home at last.

11

J.P. drove the Mercedes and Eric held me embraced in the back seat.

"How did you know when I was due to arrive?" I asked wearily.

J.P. answered, "He's been calling the airline every 15 minutes."

Eric added, "We've all been so worried. That letter you left for me wasn't as reassuring as you thought it might be. But that's all behind us now. Marianne and Dora are planning to put you to bed with warm milk and a hot water bottle as soon as we reach The Nest. We think twenty four hours of undisturbed rest will do you a lot of good. But after you've rested, I expect to hear more about this adventure of yours."

I shivered; my secret was sure to come out. I would have to use my twenty four hours of grace to get my thoughts organized and my story sanitized enough to share. Eric carried me into The Nest and into my bedroom; Zorro came tearing out of a hiding place and landed purring on my stomach before Marianne and Dora could get me undressed and settled. Don appeared bashfully proffering a bouquet of fall foliage for my bedside stand. I was embarrassed by all the attention but too tired and distraught to remonstrate. I just let it happen.

I woke about noon the next day to a tantalizing odor. Marianne was apparently a practitioner of chicken-soup medicine. I squirmed out of bed, every bone and muscle complaining, visited the bathroom for obvious reasons and tooth brushing, and arrived in the kitchen to find Marianne putting out chicken noodle soup, buttered fresh-baked bread, and a bowl of stewed peaches. She greeted me with a big hug, carefully avoiding throwing me off balance, and sat me down at the table. She brought me up to date on the children's and animals' doings while I had been away. Don had brought home another triumph, an A in math this time; Dora was in love, maybe, maybe not; Buster had bit J.P.; Pancho and Cleo had met a skunk and come out the worse for it. I was truly home again. Zorro came strolling out from under a bed somewhere, squalling for chicken.

"Dora brought that cat over to the main house while you were gone," Marianne related. "He wandered around yelling at me and beating up on Prince Peter just out of cussedness. I guess it was his way of worrying about you."

I spent the rest of the day sprawled on the sofa, drowsing in my robe and slippers, bundled in an afghan, my foot on a pillow on the coffee table. I arose about five and heated up the rest of the chicken soup, took a double dose of my pain medication, and returned to the sofa. It was dark when I heard Eric's voice echoing from the foyer.

"Are you up to company? I just thought I should look in on you."

"Come in, come in." I replied.

As I shifted my position on the sofa, the afghan and skirt of my robe fell aside from my leg, exposing the puffed and shiny evidence of its enormous swelling. Eric's reaction was instantaneous and profane.

"What the hell have you been doing? How did that leg get in that godawful shape?"

"Don't get so upset. It gets that way if I walk a lot. I'll go to the clinic tomorrow for therapy and that will take the edema down." I sounded more optimistic than I was in fact.

"I'll just bet you did a lot of walking! All those airports, changing planes! I tracked you to Albany and a rental car but after that ...."

"Tracked me? Did you think I was skipping the country? How could you track me?" I was more than a little miffed and didn't mind showing it.

"I got a friend at the airlines. What in the world were you doing in upstate New York?"

Suddenly, too much medication, too much pain, too much suppressed emotion had an effect. I burst out.

"I had to go. Woodbridge Hall notified me that my mother was dead. Woodbridge Hall is a state facility for confinement of the criminally insane. I had to go, there wasn't anyone else. She murdered a woman and two children twenty two years ago. They took her away when I was eight, but it wasn't until I was sixteen that my court-appointed guardian told me why. When I was twenty one, I could access the trial documents and learn the horrible, sickening details. Since then, in trying to forget them my mind has suppressed them, so much so that to this day I don't remember them exactly. Then last Monday, I had to remember."

There! I had finally spoken the unspeakable to someone. I had gone too far to stop. I went on. "Twenty two years ago my mother, thinking the house she invaded belonged to her supplier of drugs, confronted the innocent woman of the house. Furious at being denied drugs, she caught up a kitchen knife and stabbed the woman dead. Then she ransacked the house, found the children asleep, a boy four, a girl seven, and killed them too. She returned to Aunt Julie's house where we were living. Seeing her bloodied and raving, the knife still in her hand, Aunt Julie called the police. The police took her away. I watched from an upstairs window. I was eight years old."

Eric was watching me, his face displaying a mixture of horror and sadness. "How awful for you. How have you been able to bear the knowledge of it all these years?" He knelt by me and took both hands in his warm grasp.

I snorted and made a rueful admission. "It hasn't been hard to bear! Every time a memory threatened to surface I've put it out of my mind. Trying over and over again NOT to remember is what's been hard; mostly it has worked. There has never been any communication from her or about her in all these years. Until now, and now I've had to remember. No escape. Oh, God!"

Then the tears came in a flood. I think I cried twenty years worth in the next ten minutes. Eric rose and brought me a unopened roll of paper towels. I almost broke into hysterical laughter as I read the words on the wrapper. Super Absorbent! Wet Strength! But those features were exactly what the situation called for. While I was crying, Eric had fired up the coffee pot, and when the spate of tears had dried up a bit, he sheepishly handed me a cup of coffee. Hot and strong enough to blister paint, it was welcome and after half a cup, I was ready to face life again. Eric sat by my side, silent, holding my free hand. I felt like a fool—making such a scene, me who prided myself on my self control and unemotional approach to stress.

"I'm sorry," I apologized, handing back the coffee mug. "I don't usually act like this and I'm embarrassed to dump on you. You've been such a good friend...."

"Friends are only good if they stand by you when you need them," he responded. "Here I stand, count on me."

"Don't let the children know. I don't want them to know." Exhaustion and medication was taking its toll and I was losing touch with reality. Sinking back into the sofa's upholstered comfort, I yawned and fell instantly asleep.

12

The next morning, Buster's scream outside the window greeted the day and woke me. I was still on the sofa, covered with the afghan. Eric, who was slumped in one of the big chairs and soundly asleep, never budged. Zorro came leaping over the back of the sofa, making it plain it was his breakfast time. Oddly enough I felt a whole lot better than I had last night. Confession must be good for the soul and when the soul was at rest, the body responded. Then Dora came calling from the door on her way to litter box duty. She was puzzled to see her dad sacked out but other than a raised eyebrow, refrained from comment.

"I'll feed and water Zorro for you this morning," she said. "Do you need help getting up and ready for the day? Where's your cane?"

I thanked her, scrambled up from the sofa, and headed for the bathroom. I heard her quizzing Eric and the rumble of his answers. I hoped his explanations would satisfy her and send her on her way. By 8 A.M. I was ready for the day, dressed and breakfasted and set to leave for the clinic. I wasn't in real good shape but I was managing well enough. Eric must have been watching for me because he came up to the car just after I had levered myself into it and pretended he simply wanted to wish me a good morning. We chatted briefly. He was apparently satisfied that I could make it to the clinic on my own and so stepped back and waved me down the drive. At the clinic Paul Cohn, my therapist, pulled a grim face and plopped me in the hydrotherapy tank at once. The massage that followed was gruesomely painful but effective and I had the pleasure of seeing the dimensions of my leg show a visible decrease.

"You be here at 8:30 every day this week," Paul ordered. "Dr. MacLaren will be in his office tomorrow and I'll set up an appointment for you. I don't think you did irreparable harm to yourself but I think he ought to check you out."

Dr. MacLaren's usual good humor failed when he examined my leg and pronounced on the damage. He put me on a new course of antibiotics to forestall a potential flare-up of the infection. He changed the types and dosages of pain medication and prescribed five treatment sessions a week. He ordered construction of a new brace and more reliance on my walker. He warned me this program would last for at least two months, with an office visit every week. His face grew very serious as he cautioned that a future episode of such abuse could lead to consideration of amputation. I limped out of his office to the orthotics department fully aware of the extent and significance of the handicap I had been trying to ignore. Gritting my teeth to deal with the fitting of the new cast was only part of the determination I had to muster to face adjustments in my life style. The biggest was to acknowledge that I was a cripple, now and probably forever.

The new regimen occupied me until well after the New Year. Starting the week after Thanksgiving and lasting through the Christmas holidays heavy snowfalls kept me housebound. The kindness of J.P. and Eric managed to get me to the clinic for my weekly treatments and exams. Marianne did my grocery shopping. Early January was marked by a thaw and Dr. MacLaren's permission to relax the drug and physical therapy plan. I was back in my own car for transportation and errands. After a morning visit to the clinic in the last week of January, I decided to risk a stop at the grocery. At this early hour, competition for the handicapped parking spaces closest to the door and the electric shopping chairs was minimal. Then, groceries stowed and feeling successful about my morning achievements, I called Tyra at the art shop and asked her for a curbside visit. It was a nice day, sweater weather. We chatted for a few minutes and I ordered some acrylics since I had in mind portraying Buster in full magnificent display for the cover of the new book. Tyra said she would send them home with Dora.

"How is Dora working out?" I asked.

Tyra was enthusiastic. "She's wonderful, terrific memory for stock and customers. Always on time, asks for job-of-the-day as soon as she arrives, and that done, looks for more to do. She's the best employee I've ever had."

Then a shadow came over her face and her voice grew hesitant. "But there's something I think I should tell you. I hate doing it, it feels like I'm breaching a confidence. But I feel you should know."

"Dear me, what can be so bad?" I responded.

"It's not bad, just worrisome. Two boys have been waiting at the door for Dora every night. One of them is Davy Bonner who works after school at Baxter's print shop two doors down and across the street. Davy's a senior at Avalon Central High, the other one is his buddy, Willy something, and I don't know where he comes from. They hang around my door for ten or fifteen minutes, just larking around until Dora breaks free and goes to her car. The boys smoke but I don't think Dora does."

"What are they smoking? Pot?" I probed. Little fingers of worry jabbed at my brain. Kids these days run into so many temptations and Dora wasn't immune.

"I don't know, and I hesitate to guess because I don't want to get Dora in trouble. But sometimes I think the cigarettes look hand-rolled. I don't want to get any of them in trouble but I feel you and Dora's father should be warned. Because Dora has always gone to private school, she may be a little naïve making her friendships. But I don't want her to think I spy on her."

"Don't worry. I won't finger you but I will look into what you're telling me. Eric, Mr. Harald that is, and I thank you for your interest. Dora is very dear to him and to me too."

I was thoughtful as I drove home, stopping for a burger and fries to go, and leaving the groceries in the car when I arrived at The Nest. I planned to eat what I could save of my unhealthy but delicious lunch from Zorro's intense interest and then flop on the couch before bringing the bags in. I had reached my rest on the couch when I heard Eric at the door, arms full of brown paper bags.

"Saw these in the car and thought I'd save you a trip. How did things go today? What's the doctor saying these days?"

Although I was grateful for the assistance, I was also a little annoyed. I hated being dependent on others for help and even more I hated being considered dependent by people who helped without being asked. Then I realized how small-minded that attitude was and made an effort.

"Thanks. I appreciate your help. Dr. MacLaren has eased up on the restrictions and I confess this winter's confinement has filled my landscape portfolio quite nicely."

"So the treatments have helped."

"They have. This old leg is likely to stay attached for a while."

My tone was sharp and chilly and in my heart of hearts I was ashamed of it. Eric aimed a searching glance at the bland expression I was cultivating and then went on,

"Don't get so starchy with me, lady. I just want to be sure you're in good hands while I'm gone. I'm leaving tomorrow early for the backwoods of Ontario, taking the Hummer, big deal coming down, won't be back for two weeks. Will you be OK?"

"Of course, I'll be OK! Don and Dora in every day, J.P. and Marianne on call, I'd say I'll be in good hands!"

His reply was "Hummph!" As he stumped out, I relented and called after him,

"Take care out there in the wilds and don't worry about anything here."

I rather regretted I hadn't remembered to relate Tyra's information but on second thought decided the time wasn't right. I'd find out more while he was gone and be in a better position to tell him on his return.

13

I spent all of the next Saturday getting sketches of Buster on canvas. I put a good deal of color on before I tired. The acrylic paints made his portrait in full magnificent display strikingly brilliant. I needed still to polish some details but they could wait until tomorrow. I was rather proud of my efforts; the picture would make a terrific cover for the new book. I was resting on the sofa in the early evening when Dora appeared. She rushed in and stopped open-mouthed when she caught sight of Buster in all his glory.

"He's gorgeous, absolutely gorgeous!" she squealed. "What're you going to do with him?"

She posted herself on the opposite arm and back of the sofa, feet on the cushion, to admire him from afar while I explained about the book.

"But won't he overshadow the old-timers? That doesn't seem fair, a newcomer to the crowd to be so glorified."

"I plan to add a row of the old-timers, as you call them, across the bottom. They will be sitting in awe meeting Buster's splendor for the first time. The story line has Zorro rescuing Buster whose braggadocio has led him into cowardly behavior in the face of disaster. Although you can guess the moral of the story, I'll tell you anyway: handsome is as handsome does."

Just then, Zorro soared over the back of the couch and landed between Dora and me, hesitating, puzzled whether to come to me who set down his food bowl every day or to Dora who had overseen his kittenhood. Dora solved his dilemma by scooping him up in her arms. She seemed to welcome the diversion he had created.

"Are you home alone this evening?" I asked.

"Yes, Marianne and J.P. drove Don to play in some basketball game. They asked me if I wanted to go but I said no. Sports are so boring!" She tossed back her hair, drew a long breath, and got down to cases. "I came to ask a favor. Will you talk Dad into a new dress for the Senior Prom? I know I'm starting early to plan but I thought success might take some time. And I'm stony broke all the time just keeping my car running. He listens to you."

"No sirree. I won't talk your dad into anything. A new dress is between you and him. Have you talked to him?"

"Well, I tried and he came back with this story about a girl from a poor family he knew in high school. Her mother had scraped together the money to make her a Junior Prom dress, and when the Senior Prom came up, her mom dyed the old dress and sewed some sequins on it. Dad said the girl was the belle of the ball. I dropped the subject. I was afraid he would make me remodel the pink dress from the Harvest Dance." She flushed in embarrassment, "It isn't as if he can't afford it."

"Marianne told me how much that pink dress cost and I doubt you have finished paying for it out of your allowance. Your dad is just trying to keep you from being a spendthrift. That's what parents do." I tried hard to conceal my amusement at her dismay.

"Do you think my chances are better if I tell him I can wear it to two proms? I'm invited to the prom at our school and also to the prom at Avalon Central High. Two for one isn't such a bad deal, is it? The kids at Avalon High and Davy wouldn't know the dress was on its second round. The proms on are on different weekends."

"So you're invited to two proms. Lucky girl. Tell me about that."

"Well, there's Derek Scofield in my class. He's a big noise at school on the sports scene and has a thing for me. Everybody expected him to ask me and I accepted. He's good-looking, comes from a rich family, drives his own BMW, dresses real sharp. Wait, I got a picture of him."

She reached into her sweater pocket and pulled out a photo wallet. Derek Scofield was a handsome lad: blond curly hair, wide-set blue eyes, a candid gaze, perfect teeth in a pleasant smile.

"Very nice," I said. "Why aren't you more enthusiastic?"

She sighed. "He's short and I'll have to wear flats. And he's boring, can't talk about anything but football. Besides, I'm a lot smarter than he is."

I laughed. "Dora, honey, all your life you can expect to meet boys and men who are not as smart as you. Get used to it. When your Mr. Right comes along, you won't be giving your heart away because of his I.Q. Who's your other date?"

"Davy Bonner, he's a senior at Avalon Central. He works at Baxter's Print Shop across the square from Tyra's store. He always needs a haircut and he ought to shave every day and doesn't. His clothes are sort of tacky and he wears knockoff Nikes from Payless. He's dark-haired and dark-eyed, a head taller than me. But he reads. He just finished a book about Lincoln keeping his Cabinet together when each member thought he would make a better president than Abe. The book is called *A Team of Rivals*. I looked it over at the bookstore; it's serious reading. I know Davy's smart because Mr. Whittington handed out a challenge problem in algebra that I spent three days on without solving it. Davy did it in his head standing at Tyra's door in three minutes yesterday afternoon. I'm not sure Dad would approve of him."

"He does sound interesting and smart. Why wouldn't your dad approve?"

"I think part of why I like him is that he seems sort of dangerous. I don't mean wicked or obviously bad. But unpredictable, atypical, sort of reckless. He's got a tattoo—it's an American flag on his upper arm. His parents are divorced and he lives with his grandmother."

Then, in an abrupt change of subject, she reverted to the matter of the prom dress. "Do you suppose Dad would be more open-minded if I told him it would do for two proms? But maybe he wouldn't like me going to an Avalon High dance. I was hoping you could help me out on this."

"Dora, honey, if this is just about a new dress, hit on your dad some evening when he's relaxing after a good dinner. If it's about the boys who have asked you to the proms, why don't you work out a way to let him meet them? Maybe have a party for a few kids from your class and invite Davy and couple of his friends from his school. Spread snacks and sodas in the dining room, roll up the rugs in the living room, crank up the stereo for dancing. Tell your friends to bring their favorite CDs or whatever it is you kids are into these days. I'll back up your dad as assistant chaperone, if you like."

"That's a pretty good idea; I'll work on it. Maybe if Dad gets a chance to talk to Davy, he'll like him. He's got good manners and a nice way about him. I know Derek can sell himself on looks alone. Gee, thanks. Now I better get back home. Do you need any help before I go?"

I thanked her for her concern and sent her off.

14

Dora braced Eric at the first family dinner after his return from "the bush." As she made her case she glanced frequently at me, presumably for moral support. I was secretly amused that her words and tone had been carefully chosen to lay out a proposition thoroughly considered and maturely presented.

"Dad," she began. "A lot of the kids in my class are throwing parties these days, sort of farewell to schooldays stuff. You know, you've been letting me go to the ones where the parents are on the scene. I was thinking it's maybe about time to invite some of my friends to a party here. What do you think?"

"Sounds OK," Eric responded cautiously, well aware Dora was working up to a proposal and that she had discussed it with me ahead of time. "But as I must remind you, the devil's always in the details. Let me in on your plan. If it rises to my standards, I'll consider it."

"Nothing fancy, Dad, nothing in any way naughty. You know I don't go for stuff like that. I was thinking a Friday or Saturday evening; twelve, maybe fifteen kids, boys and girls. And I was intending to invite Don so he could ask that girl he likes so much; he's old enough to come to a grownup teen party. I already talked to Marianne and she says if it's OK with you, it's OK with her especially if I do most of the work. Just snacks and sodas in the dining room, music and DVD's in the living room, rugs rolled up for dancing. You and Thena would be welcome to make the scene."

Eric's response was firm but kindly. "You bet Thena and I would make the scene. There won't be a gang of teens in this house without chaperones." He continued by raising a quizzical eyebrow and posing a question. "This age category you're calling 'grownup teens' is new to me. Would you mind explaining?"

Don burst out laughing and joined the conversation. "Grownup teens is what the high school seniors at our school call themselves when they want to do something parents or teachers won't approve of. Rumor has it grownup teen parties are big on beer, petting, and pot."

Eric was quick to follow up. "Dora! Do the parties you go to feature liquor? Or big time petting? Or smoking?"

"Oh, Dad," Dora was wide-eyed in denial. "You don't think I would do anything like that, do you?"

"Not on your own, I don't, but kids in a crowd can stray from standards of behavior I consider appropriate. Any party you might have would have to go by the rules. When you invite your friends tell them there will be no liquor, tobacco, or pot on the premises and anyone that tries to bring it will be turned away at the door. That, and they should plan to leave at midnight or before. Now, would someone please pass the butter?"

Dinner table conversation resumed without Eric having given explicit approval of Dora's party plans. But when dessert (one of Marianne's to-die-for German chocolate cakes) arrived Dora raised the subject again.

"Well, Dad, do I have your permission for a party or not? I think I can make your rules stick. The friends I expect to invite are pretty mature, not rowdy or given to misbehavior."

Don interjected again, "If they're all like that Derek Scofield and his All-American football buddies, the party may turn into a prayer meeting." He raised his hands to sketch out a square in the air. "I'm pretty sick of coach telling us we should be more like Derek. He never cusses, he's always on time, he embodies team spirit, he's ...."

Dora cut him off, "Oh, shut up! He's boring but he's a nice guy and a good dancer. You as a lowly junior are not qualified to pass judgment on a senior whose invitation to the prom I've accepted."

Eric intervened. "Enough of the bickering. Dora, you can have your party subject to the rules I've laid down. I'll expect you to help in the preparations and to clean up after and to behave with good sense and good manners throughout. Agreed?"

He might have said more but Dora's gratitude had him in a bear hug that muffled further comment. Later, as I was gathering up my cane and starting for the door to return to The Nest, Dora wrapped me in a hug and whispered in my ear,

"Thanks for the idea. He's not such an ogre after all, is he?"

I chuckled and left her already engrossed in plans. The sole topic of conversation in the Harald household became party, party, party. I was confidante to every aspect, from what to wear to the best arrangement of living room furniture. I listened patiently although something arose to occupy my mind .

When I returned from Troy Junction, I had placed Alicia's box of trinkets and packet of letters in a bureau drawer and had thereafter deliberately forgotten them. A kind of a vague aversion to handling Alicia's things deterred my investigation. But one day, the sun was shining, my painting was going well, my spirits were high, and the pain in my leg was less than usual. Considering a walk, I dipped into the bureau drawer for a scarf to tie down my hair. Then moved by an ill-defined impulse, part curiosity, part revulsion, I took out the box and packet and carried them to the kitchen table.

The box was painted tin, lined with frayed velvet stretched over crumbling padding. That day in my motel room in Troy Junction, I had removed the lid just long enough to glimpse the contents. Now I examined each item. The first was a rhinestone pin one might wear on the lapel of a suit and shaped as an "A". I tried to lift out a long string of cut glass beads, black and clear beads interspersed, but the string, rotted by time, broke in my hand and individual beads tumbled back into the box. Two rings lay in the jumble, one a small opal set on either side with tiny green stones, the other a plain gold band. Inscribed on the inside of the gold band were an A and an R intertwined and a date: May 4, 1970. Alicia's wedding ring? Six years before I was born? This was a puzzle, I knew that my birth certificate bore only my mother's name, the space for a father's name was blank. Had Alicia indeed been married before I was born? Married to a mysterious "R" recorded on the inside of the ring? Was "R" my unrecorded father? I was ruminating questions that I wasn't sure I wanted answered.

I laid aside the rings and began to pick out loose beads and place them in a shallow bowl. Probing a bulge in the lining on one side of the box, I extracted a bundle of pawn tickets. The tickets were for a guitar, a wrist watch, a diamond solitaire, a table radio, three bracelets on separate tickets, a gold chain, a cameo, a pair of diamond earrings, and a locket. Spreading out the tickets and arranging them chronologically, I saw the amounts realized from the pawn were generally modest and strung out over some three years prior to the time of Alicia's crime. Either the quality of the items pawned was paltry or Alicia failed to bargain for best dollar. My initial guess that the pawn had fed her addiction seemed flawed; small proceeds would scarcely have supported a serious drug habit. Then I remembered something I had read in the transcript of her trial. She had been employed as a data entry clerk for the electric company, had a good work record, and had been paid regularly. Examining psychiatrists ascribed motivation for her murderous behavior to a schizophrenic brainstorm triggered by an acute, excessive, single, mixed dose of illicit drugs, followed by an intractable psychosis. The defense lawyer had argued her aberrant behavior was a recreational event gone wrong. A plea of diminished capacity based on the psychiatric diagnosis spared her the sentence of capital punishment; she was sentenced to life imprisonment in an institution for the criminally insane. I wished I could reread the trial transcript, I wished I could ask questions of Aunt Julie and Uncle George, I wished I could talk to the pawn shop owner and look at his records, I wished I knew why she needed money so badly.... I wished I had never ventured on this train of thought. Although I wasn't sure what I wished, I was nevertheless sure there was more to know than I had ever known about Alicia Bonham.

I returned the baubles to the box and took up the packet of letters. There were 18 letters still in their envelopes, many unopened. The cancellation imprints were for cities in Alaska. I arranged them in chronologic order. Some of the cancellations were too smudged to be sure of the dates, although they seemed to fall at two or three week intervals during a couple of years before Alicia's crime. The letters were all addressed in the same clumsy hand to Aunt Julie's house; none bore a return address. My breath was coming quick and my hands were shaking as I took a table knife from the kitchen drawer and lifted the flap of the envelope of the earliest letter. On a single sheet of lined paper from a cheap tablet, the penciled message began,

> *Dear A*
>
> *Just a line to let you know I started the job yesterday. I think it will be good. I like the boss and my mates seem to be good joes. We're still in town but going out to the job sight first thing tomorrow morning. Maybe I won't be able to write often. The guys tell me mail pickup is irregalar. I gave you the address of the company the last time I saw you. I hope you use it often. Hearing from you will always make my day, even when night is 6 months long. Ha! Ha! Tell Thena I will bring her a present when I get back. Love to you both, R*

All the letters followed pretty much the same format. They seemed to indicate a man of imperfect education and limited imagination. The third letter in the series said "Red letter day. Your letter was very welcome. I wish you kept the money I sent. Hope Thena's tonsilextomy goes OK." After that letter after letter said little more than "I'm fine, hope you are the same" and "wish I would hear from you." Although he referred more than once to sending money there was only the single mention that Alicia had responded with an acknowledgment. The letters were generally uninteresting although once R reported he saw a bear and another announced "Ken lost a finger to the chain saw today." He corresponded faithfully during the period covered by the letters but none contained a clue as to a formal relationship with Alicia or me. They might as well have originated from a mere acquaintance or a distant relative. I had an impression of R as an unskilled worker on a construction project out in the boondocks. Unopened letters became more common and then a constant for the last five in the series. Alicia, it seemed, had no incentive nor opportunity to open them.

As I laid down the last letter, I straightened from my hunched posture and rubbed my aching neck. R's handwriting was fairly good but he used a soft lead pencil and flimsy paper and many words blurred. I peered hard at each and every word, hoping to find even the slightest clue to R's identity or his connection to me and Alicia. At last I slowly restored each of the letters to its envelope and stacked them, carefully squaring the corners. I tried to retie the scrap of pink ribbon around them but it fell apart in my fingers. My fingers felt like wooden sticks as I handled the packet and slipped it inside a large manila envelope. That done, I looked up from my task in surprise, expecting to see gloom and dark clouds outside the big windows but the day was still gloriously sunny, the birds were still singing, the flowers were still bobbing in the spring breeze. The gloom was inside me. What was I going to do now?

15

I gave up on a walk. Instead I took a sketch pad and handful of charcoal pencils and went over to the main house. Sketching Oscar would be a good distraction. The house was very quiet, only Oscar's raucous greetings broke the silence. No one else was home; Eric was out in the bush somewhere, the kids were in school, Marianne and J.P. were taking the afternoon for a movie in town. I settled down to my task while Oscar obliged by strolling up and down along his perch, fanning his crest and furling and unfurling his wings. I caught a number of excellent poses and began to consider quitting for the day. As I sketched the stylized monogram of my signature, a random memory floated though my mind. I remembered asking my mother once, "Why am I Athena?" and her answer, "She was a woman wise and brave, such as I hope you will be." I had stopped to think about that when suddenly I heard the mud room door slam and then a howl of anguish. That had to be Don. I leaped up and thinking he might be hurt, made my way at my best speed to the mud room. The first thing I saw was Don's backpack thrown down by the coat rack, books and papers spilling out of it, and Don sitting on the floor in Arthur's bed, the dog's motionless golden body pulled across his lap. Rocking back and forth, he was moaning and choking on tears and sobs. Seeing me, he cried out,

"He's dead, he's dead. He was all right this morning when I left and now he's dead. Why didn't anybody know?"

I realized then that I had been the last to see Arthur alive. When I came in, he had risen, pushed his nose into my hand, and then returned to his bed.

"Are you sure he's dead? He greeted me when I came over just a couple of hours ago."

"He's dead, he's dead. I know. I can tell. I put my ear to his chest and his heart's not beating. His tongue's just lopping out of his mouth and there's no breath coming out of his mouth or nose. It must have just happened, he's still warm. Can't we do CPR or something? Maybe if we get the vet to come...."

My game leg made me helpless to comfort him while he was down on the floor. I just stood there trying to think of a way to help him bear this terrible loss. He clutched Arthur's body more tightly and lifted his grief-distorted, tear-besmeared face to tell me,

"I got Arthur for my puppy when I was three years old. I fed and watered him and brushed him and I even sneaked him into my bed sometimes. He always came when I called, now he's dead and he'll never be with me any more. What am I gonna do? When Momma died, I told him and he licked my tears. He knew, he knew all about me, good times and bad."

I finally put aside my cane and made the effort to slide my body down the door jamb until I too was on the floor where I could reach over and hold both boy and dog in my arms. Arthur was a big dog and Don was a big boy and it was a stretch to get my arms around the two of them. But just being close seemed to help Don. He reached for a corner of Arthur's blanket and mopped his face, then sneezed as loose hair tickled his nose. I was crying too. We huddled there for 20 minutes or so before J.P. and Marianne came home and found us. J.P. helped me to my feet, then he and Marianne untangled Don from Arthur's body and coaxed him to the sofa in the family room. Poor kid! the excess of female consolation, Marianne on one side, me on the other, added to his embarrassment until he managed to get his emotions under control. Then Dora arrived and J.P. brought her up to speed as she came through the mud room. Rushing at Don in her typically impetuous fashion, she threw her arms around him in a smothering hug.

"Oh, Dondo, Dondo, I'm so sorry, so sorry," she cried.

Her tears started his all over again, but he replied gruffly and started to wriggle out of her embrace to reply. "For Pete's sake, don't call me that baby name. And let go of me. I got to go to the bathroom." As he got himself free, he growled, "Why is it the people we love and that love us got to die? Do you know?"

Dora rose and followed him out of the room. I heard her say, "Hey, it happens. We can't do anything about it. All we can do is remember and love one another all the more."

The bathroom door slammed on her philosophy. I decided Don was in good hands and went to the kitchen to pick up my sketches. Marianne invited me to supper but I had leftovers back at The Nest and declined. "No thanks. Has anyone called Eric?"

"J.P. reached him over in Perry County. He'll be home later this evening. That should help Don deal with things. Poor kid. His mother's loss was so hard for him and now Arthur…." She dabbed a tear from her eye with a Kleenex. Don's losses were hers as well.

I was beginning to feel an intruder in this family tragedy. Dora seemed at the moment the best medicine for Don. It was time for me to leave. I told Marianne to call if I could help. She nodded and I left.

Around nine o'clock, I was coddling my aches and pains in my robe and slippers on the sofa when Eric called out from the door. I welcomed him in. His worry was written all over his face. "It's too bad about Arthur; he was Don's lifelong companion but he had to be 13 almost 14 years old. I just hope Don doesn't take it too hard. He's not good with death and dying. Dora seemed to handle Mary's sickness and death in a fairly reasonable way, but it hit Don very, very hard. I don't know why he was so much more affected than Dora."

"Dora was older, not by much but enough. And she told me Mary had prepared her for the inevitable. Don didn't have those advantages. He told me once that Mary never admitted to him that she was in pain. He knew she was dying, wanted to share her pain, but didn't know how and she didn't help him. I think he resented that and felt guilty that she didn't confide in him and rely on him. I'm optimistic that he'll be able to handle the loss of Arthur with more ease. He's more mature and although Arthur was very dear to him, he was after all only a pet "

Eric responded with what seemed a *non sequitur,*

"You know that statue of the cupbearers: Don hates it passionately and I'm beginning to understand why. We had gone to New York and had just spent the day at Sloan Kettering getting the bad news about Mary's tumor. She sent me back to the hotel saying that she wanted to walk alone in the park for a while. When she came back to the room, she told me she had bought something, When I wanted to know what, all she would say was, 'It's an affirmation of life, wait until it's delivered at home.' Well, when we opened the crate and put aside the packing, Mary set the statue on the end table and gathered Don and Dora in her arms on the sofa to tell them the statue was a tribute to the loveliness of their youth and her love for them. Then she told the two of them what the doctors had said. Neither of the children had much to say. They just hugged and kissed her and went off very soberly to their rooms. For Don that statue must be a symbol of Mary's inescapable loss. Poor kid, it must remind him every time he passes it. I've got to get rid of it."

"Don't be in such a hurry. You're probably right that he associates it with the awful news he had that day and that he blames it for the loss of his mother. But he has grown to understand that it had meaning for Mary. Learning that it has no meaning for him will take more time. But the healing won't continue if you remove it from his world. It needs to be there for him to accept all the feelings he associates with it."

I felt like a fool, pontificating as I was, while privately struggling with the feelings that a dead woman's legacy of pawn tickets and letters had roused in me. In that instant, I made a conscious decision to pursue answers to the questions that Alicia's things had raised. I, too, needed to heal, and ignoring Alicia's life wasn't the way to achieve the healing I needed. The turmoil of conflicting thoughts must have marked my face because Eric reached over and touched my hand.

"Thank you, Thena," he said. "I cherish your insights and your interest in my children. Now, it's late and bed is in order for both of us."

He rose and coming around the back of the sofa, bent down to my upturned face and gently kissed my lips. I went thoughtfully off to bed and fell asleep with Zorro purring between my feet.

16

The next morning I looked out from my kitchen window to watch a small procession—two men and a boy silhouetted against the bright eastern sky—the boy carrying the shrouded body of his best friend, the men armed with shovels and spades. They trudged along the crest of a long rise running a third of a mile from the barn to an ancient silver maple overlooking the eastern meadow. The valley below the rise lay dark, the light of the rising sun blocked by the hill. Leaves of the maple tree caught the sun and shivered silver and green in a gentle breeze. Arriving at the tree Don put down his burden and joined Eric and J.P. to dig a grave at its foot. After Don had laid Arthur away in the pit, the three of them filled it in and tamped down the loose earth. They stood for a few long minutes, Eric with his hand on the boy's shoulder. Then three men walked slowly back toward the house, Don's boyhood ended by a rite of passage.

I was restless and decided baking cookies would be a good occupation for a Saturday morning. I was no cook but I had picked up from Marianne half a dozen never-fail recipes. I was just taking the last batch of oatmeal nuggets from the oven when Don called from the door.

"Smells like cookies! Boy, am I hungry! I just finished feeding Pancho and Cleo and grooming all the horses."

"Go wash your face and hands and I'll fix you up with warm cookies and milk."

I was relieved to see a cheerful face and normal appetite. We sat down at the table and chatted about the animals that lived in the barn. Suddenly, he put down his empty milk glass and posed a question.

"Is there some place where the souls of animals go when they die? You know, like people heaven?"

I certainly had no answer for that. I wasn't even sure I believed in a people heaven, much less an animal heaven. So I shared a childhood memory.

"When I was a little kid, I read a book that I think was called *Beautiful Joe's Paradise*. I don't remember all the details but Beautiful Joe was a dog that had died after a hard life of want and abuse. He had been given the job of running a place where deserving animals went after they died. Beautiful Joe's Paradise was a lovely place with lots of good things to eat, perfect weather, and comfortable places to lie and sit in the sun and tell stories of past lives. Of the horses, dogs, and cats enjoying the Paradise some had very sad stories to tell of a cruel life but others told of happy lives with kind and loving masters and mistresses. I knew very well it was just a fantasy but I wanted to believe it. Maybe I still want to. But it's up to you to accept or reject a fantasy of your own. I know that if Arthur were to end up in Beautiful Joe's Paradise, he would speak only good of his life with you."

Don absorbed this tale with courteous attention, sat thoughtful for a moment, and then asked, "Can I have another glass of milk?"

He left soon after, whistling cheerfully. The batch of cookies had been decimated.

Dora's week was a flurry of preparations for her party. As she had promised Eric she did all the work herself. Marianne and I were nevertheless frequently consulted for our advice and opinions. She shopped for her supplies at the supermarket, draining her allowance, and lugged in cases of soda and bags of chips. She baked brownies and two kinds of cookies and stirred up salsa and a selection of dips. She sought frequent reassurance that she would have enough food, citing the horrible example of Trudie Gershon's party: the chips had run out by ten o'clock and all the kids had for the dips was stale soda crackers! Marianne told her to quit worrying, she would have enough for an army. The morning of the party, she made dozens of ham and cheese sandwiches, carefully cutting off the crusts. When I expressed surprise at a large platter of crudités she was arranging, she explained that a health food kick had swept the school. A platter of fresh fruit—pineapple, kiwi, and green and red grapes—increased the variety of choices. Marianne told me the current fad for healthy food stemmed from an appearance of a stunningly svelte female nutritionist at a recent school convocation. If chronically insouciant teenagers had been converted to healthy food choices, that nutritionist must have made a powerful impression indeed.

Dora got J.P. and Don to roll up the rugs in the family room and personally supervised the arrangement of the furniture, the supply of DVDs and CDs, and removal of the more fragile of Mary's trimmings to the formal living room. At six o'clock on party day, she scurried to shower, wash her hair, and dress in her best jeans and shirt. I told her it was a mistake to get ready so early, it gave her too much time to worry. But she informed me, "A person can't worry too much about a party. Everything has got to be perfect. If it's not, people talk. Trudie's party was in February and the girls are still talking about it."

17

By eight o'clock Dora and Don were posted at the door to greet guests; Don was grumbling under his breath because she had sent him to change his shirt twice. He had, however, regained his good humor before the first guests began to straggle in. On arrival the boys and girls were shunted for introductions to where Eric and I had been stationed next to the fireplace. Dora's classmates on the whole were a well-groomed bunch sporting designer jeans, shirts, and shoes, nothing too outré. I guessed at conservative parents exerting control over clothing purchases. Davy Bonner brought another fellow and a girl. They were as fashionable but in a totally different genre. I suspected the girl, Pansy something, had dressed for shock value; her tight jersey top stopped short just below her breasts and her low-slung jeans disclosed a stud sparkling in her navel. An excess of makeup was further accentuated by studs in her nose, ears, lip, and eyebrow. Davy and his male friend wore what I was beginning to recognize as a teenage uniform in some quarters: long baggy shorts, loose sports jerseys, baseball caps, and jogging shoes.

Don's date, Tiffany Pardee, and the famous Derek Scofield held my particular interest from the start. Tiffany was petite, shy, and very pretty in an old-fashioned way, pale lipstick her only makeup, wide blue eyes, and blonde Shirley Temple curls. Derek lived up to the photo I had seen of him and to Dora's description; his manners were beautiful and

69

his grooming impeccable but he was indeed short. He soon became the nexus of an adoring group savoring a week-old victory in field hockey; Derek had starred and scored and now preened. When Don and Dora started the dancing, Tiffany forgot her shyness to gyrate in the latest moves. I overheard Don say her sister brought the hottest dances home from college. Davy's friend and Pansy promptly joined in the dancing but Davy hung back. I noticed that he was inspecting titles on the book wall.

With the party well on its way, Eric and I retired to the formal living room and sat with books in hand, each of us with one ear cocked to monitor the hubbub in the family room. I noticed a lively traffic to the spread in the dining room and around 9:30 I made a quick trip to check on things out there. Dora was managing to keep up with the ravages of teenage appetites so far; backup plates of sandwiches and veggies had made their appearance and the bowls of chips and tub of iced drinks were still well-furnished. I encountered Davy alone and hovering over the table; I wondered if he was hiding out. Contrary to Dora's description, he was well shaved and showed the effects of a recent haircut. Heavy dark brows shadowed his face but sharp grey eyes glowed between long curling lashes over high cheekbones. I could understand Dora's use of the word "dangerous." He was quite tall, maybe three or four inches over six feet, and he carried himself with a kind of lanky grace. Seeing me, he volunteered a conversation,

"You must be Ms. Bonham. I like your drawings," he said. "I gave my little sister the book about the animals for Christmas; the turtle is her favorite. I wish I could draw and paint but Avalon Central shut down the art program when the school appropriation got cut."

"I'm pleased that my work has pleased you and your sister. It's just happenstance that I do art for a living. My education was in biology with a minor in art. What do you plan for a career?" I asked.

"I want to be a doctor. They make lots of money and help people too. But the counselor says I ought to aim for something else, because my aptitudes test for mechanical skills. I really like art and science but I'll probably end up as a car mechanic." His words had a bitter twist and his dark face darkened further.

"Dora tells me you are very bright. I would think you could easily get scholarships for college. Doing well in college would be a step toward admission to medical school. A friend of mine told me that it was easier to get into medical school than into college; sponsors and subsidies abound for well-qualified candidates, especially those with abilities in math and science."

"Did Dora talk about me to you?"

"Yes, she told me you had read *Team of Rivals*. I just finished it and I admire your choice of reading material. It's a really good book and Goodwin is a really good historian, don't you think?"

"Yeah, I got it at the library. Say, could I ask Dora to bring me some time to see how you draw the animals?"

"Of course." I said.

Just then our *tête-à-tête* was interrupted by an influx of hungry, thirsty kids and Davy drifted off to the family room again. When I returned to the living room, I said to Eric, "Keep an eye out for Davy Bonner; he's holing up in the dining room. He either doesn't dance or he's shy around Dora's classmates. You'll enjoy talking to him."

When Eric looked puzzled, I continued, "He's the kid who invited Dora to the Avalon Central High prom."

"Oh, yes. I'd like to talk to him, find out what he's like. That Scofield kid is a double-barreled bore, even if he does end every sentence with a 'sir.' Good-lookin' though."

Honoring Dora and Don's curfew, the guests had gone by 11:30, and clearing away in the dining room was in progress. With the music turned off, the silence in the house was deafening, broken only by an occasional exchange between the children as they put away leftovers and loaded the dishwasher. Eric and I held a brief post mortem as I bid him good night at the door.

"I think the party was a success, don't you? A bunch of nice kids, well-behaved," I said. "They seemed to have a good time."

"Yes," Eric replied. "Say, I did get a chance to talk to Davy Bonner. He's something else. We actually had a conversation. He asked me what I did for a living. When I said I brokered lumber and wood products, he asked me whether I thought the new cement clapboards and roof shingles would make a dent in the wood products business. I said not yet but the guy at the last seminar I attended was taking them very seriously for their fire-retardant characteristics. Davy came back with examples of effectiveness in the latest California firestorms. We had just proceeded to current standards of suburban construction when a couple of other kids came in and Davy retreated to the family room. I tell you, that kid will either end up a gangster or CEO of a Fortune 500 company."

"Why a gangster?" I asked.

"On looks alone. He's got a intense, unpredictable air about him."

I departed, chuckling, for The Nest.

18

The Harald place returned to its wonted peace and quiet now that Dora's party was over. My thoughts in the bleak hours of the night and empty hours of the day became free to dwell on Alicia's pawn tickets and the letters from R. I finally concluded that to allay the doubts and fears nagging at me, I had to drive to Yonkers and talk to Aunt Julie and maybe to Uncle George. I was sitting on the deck with an atlas planning my route and making notes to call for motel reservations when Eric appeared, rosy and panting from his morning jog.

"It's a great day!" he called out. "If you've got any coffee, I'll join you."

"Sure, in the kitchen. Help yourself. I've had mine."

He returned to the deck with his cup and slouched into one of the chairs. Noticing my atlas, he asked,

"Going somewhere?"

We seemed to be safely alone so I told him what I had found when I went through Alicia's things and that my intention was to find out more about them. He responded carefully, weighing his words.

"You seem to be taking this new information pretty calmly. Maybe it's not a bad idea to pursue the leads it gives you. However, I hope you are preparing yourself for bad as well as good outcomes. Sometimes digging into the past, especially someone else's past, can be like opening

Pandora's box. Didn't that female's curiosity let all of mankind's evils loose on our world?"

"I've thought of that. But what can be worse than what I already know? Maybe knowing more will explain Alicia's madness, maybe I can learn to forgive it, maybe I'll learn who R is or was, and how he connected to Alicia. I've concluded further probing is worth a shot, whatever it turns up."

Eric nodded, his face grave. "I can't tell you whether your plan is right or wrong. It's your life and your problem to work out. All I can say is that you can count on me should you need my help. Have you got plenty of money? I mean, in case you want to hire detectives or anything? I hope you won't come back from this junket as damaged as you did from the last."

"I hardly think my inquiries will require gumshoes. And if it does, I can handle it. The Harald menagerie has provided me with a generous income, you know. I thought I'd tell the family I'm going to New York to see publishers, sightsee, and see a show or two. I'm going to drive and you can expect me back in a week or so."

Eric's expression turned sour. "I suppose you'll hook up with that guy Pattison while you're there?"

"Maybe." I was non-committal and my tone diverted Eric from further comment.

I continued with preparations for the trip, had the car serviced, packed a bag with clothes for a week on the road, and arranged with Dora to look after Zorro. The family took my announcement in its stride, except for Dora. Her first reaction was worry that I would not be home to see her off to her proms and to attend graduation ceremonies at her school. I assured her I expected to make it back in time. I didn't say so but I intended to make my visit to Yonkers as short and as sweet as possible.

I left on Monday morning. Travelling the monotony of superhighways gave me a lot of time for thinking and rethinking but failed to lead me to any conclusions. I pulled up at the Yonkers Ramada in the late afternoon on Tuesday. My first move after registering was to consult a phone book for Aunt Julie's name and address. Both had remained the same since I last saw her. When I reached her that evening, she recognized my voice without enthusiasm or obvious surprise. I arranged to drop by the house about ten the next morning. I braced myself for the encounter.

Aunt Julie's house hadn't changed, an old brownstone row house with a curlicue iron balustrade on the shallow steps of the stoop. Full length lace curtains looped up with satin cord still decked the tall narrow windows that looked out over window boxes planted with red and pink geraniums and white and purple alyssum. The door opened almost before I took my finger off the bell button. Aunt Julie stood there, taller and heavier than I remembered her, white streaks in her hair and deep wrinkles around her dark eyes. She was a big woman, and her expressionless gaze and toneless voice were forbidding once she spoke.

"You haven't changed," she said. "You can come in." She stepped back and opened the door wider.

I wasn't sure what to say. After ten years, "Hello" seemed inadequate, but anything more seemed fulsome. So I didn't say anything, just stepped inside and followed her into the parlor. Shining clean, the room was furnished in well-kept Danish modern, totally out of keeping with the period and style of the house.

"You have new furniture in here." I ventured. "It's very nice."

"I got married to a man who works for a living. He likes nice things and is willing to spend money on them. What have you been doing? The only word I've had from you in all these years is a birthday card now and then and a Christmas card every year."

Her voice conveyed neither approval nor disapproval of my shortcomings in correspondence. But I was stung by her implied criticism.

"I don't recall even that much from you," I retorted.

"You can sit down. Maybe you can tell me why you've turned up now."

Despite the prickly tone of her words, her face remained deadpan and her eyes lay like black pebbles under her brows. I didn't sense active malevolence but at the same time, I wasn't getting friendly vibes. She was making me feel like an undesirable object, like doggy-doo on the sidewalk. Nevertheless I didn't remember Aunt Julie ever being ruthless even when disciplining me. I remembered occasional punishments— sitting in the corner, going without dinner, no TV for a week, for instance—but she had never raised a hand to me. Her punishments were dispensed with a cold passionless indifference, as if she were performing an unpleasant duty according to rules laid down in a book. Never a hint of affection, never a well-done. Conversation limited to need-of-the-now to get through the day, the week, the year. Perhaps the best description of our old relationship was mutual and dutiful indifference. Now I was beginning to feel that her present attitude was somewhat different from the one I knew of old. She had always seemed imposing to me, dominating, but until now not intimidating. Well, I was a big girl now and not about to be dominated or intimidated. I gathered my resolve and got right down to business.

"Alicia's dead. Last September. I had her buried in Troy Junction where the institution is. They gave me her things, but I didn't look at them until a few weeks ago. There was a little jewel box mostly containing pawn tickets and a packet of letters tied with a ribbon."

"I know. I put that stuff and an outfit in a suitcase so she had something decent to wear to court. The prosecutor took the rest of her stuff and never gave it back. He let your stuff alone."

"How did it happen that she and I lived here?"

"She came to work where I did, said she needed a place for her and her kid to live. My first husband was a deadbeat; when we split, he wouldn't pay the alimony I was awarded. I needed money and this house was mine, inherited from my grandparents, and I had a spare room. You were four, and she worked nights and I worked days so between us there was somebody in the house all the time. It wasn't charity, she paid board and room for the two of you."

"If she had a job, she must have had an income. Why did she have to hock stuff? Did she ever say she was short of money?" I wondered.

"We didn't talk, she lived her life and I lived mine."

As if locking a door on speech, Aunt Julie closed her lips firmly over her teeth. Her gaze flickered away from mine and she shifted slightly in her chair. Was I sensing evasion?

"You must have spent some time together, Saturdays, Sundays."

"I was always away on weekends, visiting my son at my parents' house. I don't know what Allie did."

"Did you know she did drugs?

"Wondered sometimes but never knew for sure. She must've, seein' as how that's what made her kill them folks." A secretive look flitted over her face, like a ripple on smooth water when a water creature comes near the surface without breaking it..

I was getting nowhere with Aunt Julie. I couldn't believe she had been totally disconnected from Alicia. But I had a hunch she wanted me to think so. My conviction grew that she knew something but was stubbornly refusing to share it.

"Did you?" I ventured.

"Did I what?" she snapped.

"Do drugs?"

Fierce anger flared in her eyes, but her answer when it came was a grim NO.

"You better go. I'm done answering questions about Allie. I had my fill when the lawyers were preparing the case."

She rose and so did I. I followed her to the door and left without further words. I thought I would try for answers to Alicia's past elsewhere before pursuing them with Aunt Julie.

19

After bite of lunch, I started for Uncle George's office. I knew my chances of seeing him were poor; I should have phoned for an appointment but I thought I would gamble. As it turned out, he was in, not engaged, and willing to see me.

Uncle George's office was also as I remembered it, a store front in a back street of a run down neighborhood more notable for the number of its ethnic groceries than for cultural amenities. The immediate environment of Uncle George's office had changed but not the genre: a pizza parlor had taken over Goldstein's candy store; Kinsey's Soul Food offered its wares in the old store that once was Danilov's Uptown Grocery; The Love of God Congregation occupied the premises of Lubitsch's Kosher Meat Market. I entered the office through a glass door with the painted but peeling legend "Geo ge K. Dempsey, At rney at Law" and identified myself to a lackadaisical blue-haired lady with glasses dangling from a bead necklace over her chest. She announced my name and arrival on a dusty intercom and then waved me into a back room.

Uncle George heaved himself out of his chair to greet me and seat me in the client's chair. He too had grown—in girth, gray hair, and wrinkles. I remembered him in his youthful 40s, thick dark hair, bright blue eyes, and quick incisive speech. Now the dark hair was reduced to a tonsure, the blue eyes were rheumy, and his diction was perceptibly slurred. I wondered if there was a pint bottle of whiskey in a desk drawer. But he didn't smell of liquor and his greeting was cordial. We caught one another up to date since our last meeting some twelve years ago. Having been diagnosed with high blood pressure and diabetes a couple of years ago, he had turned most of his practice to divorce cases. Less demanding, he said. I filled in the events in my life, although he was not surprised by them since insurance companies, prospective employers, and Woodbridge Hall had been in frequent or recent contact with him.

"I've just been to see Julie Corbin," I said. "I came upon some things of my mother that raised some questions I hoped she could answer."

"Not Corbin any more, Hasselhoff. New husband, but she's kept her old name. I don't know why. Did she have anything useful to tell you?"

"Well, I was going to ask about a batch of pawn tickets and a packet of letters, Alicia's things that Woodbridge Hall turned over to me. But Julie got so defensive and even offensive that I backed off. Rather than make her more hostile, I thought I would try you for information."

I pulled the bundle of pawn tickets and the packet of letters out of my purse and laid them on Uncle George's desk. He leafed through the pawn tickets quickly and read the letters carefully. He looked up with a question.

"Any idea who this R is or was?"

"I was hoping you would know."

"Nothing comes to mind. But the pawn tickets make some sense. Alicia was always in a financial bind. She made barely enough to pay Julie room and board for the two of you. Yet you were always dressed like a little princess, always had the latest toy or book, and got treated to events such as the IceCapades, the circus, or the Civic Theatre's *Nutcracker* performance. My guess is that she got the money for that kind of thing at the hock shop."

"Wasn't she thought to be feeding an addiction to coke and meth? But when I went over these pawn tickets, I couldn't make the trifling amounts she got from them jibe with extensive drug purchases. Your suggestion makes a lot more sense. What do you know about her addiction?" I was growing more puzzled by the moment.

Dempsey (I was making a conscious effort to drop the Uncle George) shifted to a more comfortable position in his chair. I sensed I was about to learn more both in quantity and quality from him than from Ms. Hasselhoff.

"You were just a baby when we met. I never knew she was addicted, although I knew some of her friends had disreputable habits. To explain, I'll have to fill you in a bit as to my life. Twenty five years ago, I was riding high, respected in my profession, making good money, married to a wonderful girl. Her family was studded with successful lawyers, father a judge, grandfather, uncle, and two brothers practicing as a prestigious firm; naturally her husband was expected to join up. Well, I did. But after a few years I broke free to set up a personal practice down here where I thought people needed good but affordable lawyering. You may have suspected this practice doesn't pull down the kind of money my wife was used to and breaking up with the family firm meant breaking up with her. We had no children and the divorce was amicable. But I began to slide into depression; my in-laws had labeled me a failure and I started to believe it. I began to drink too much and fell in with Alicia's crowd. I was hitting bottom with a lot of alcohol, some coke, some Ecstasy. Alicia talked me into AA and AA counselors talked me into treatment for clinical depression. In a way, I think of Alicia as the savior of my physical and mental health. We were never more than friends and neither of us had time for socializing a lot. After she moved into Julie's house, we met and talked infrequently. She was working weekends as a waitress; most of her additional income went to pay for baby-sitting for you since Julie never stayed home on weekends. I never knew whether she used drugs recreationally or if she had an addiction but I didn't know her well enough to rule out the possibility. I do know you were the center of her universe. When she got in trouble, I did what I could, but that's another story."

"Julie sounds something of a villain in Alicia's story. I wondered whether she was hiding something. Do you think there's something more to her hostility than disgust with lawyers' questioning?"

"Don't read too much into what I'm about to say. I've always had a hunch Julie was more involved in Alicia's tragedy than we could learn at the time. When I met Alicia, she knew about AA because she had been briefly married to a drunk and quickly divorced to escape spousal abuse. She arrived in Yonkers from a country town upstate, with a couple of suitcases and you, a three-month-old baby. She was working in a McDonald's and child care cost was eating up her income when she happened to stop in here to ask about Aid to Dependent Children. She didn't tell me anything about her marriage but I got a notion that you were the result of a temporary and thoroughly unsatisfactory liaison. I don't know what she told the social worker who set up ADC for her. I do know the father line on your birth certificate is blank. Somehow I have always thought Julie took advantage of some vulnerability that Alicia was concealing."

"Alicia had a wedding ring, inscribed A and R intertwined and a date May 4, 1970." I mused aloud. "That seems to jibe with a marriage made when she was very young, long before I was born. Could the R of the letters be the same man, re-entering her life apparently unwelcomed twenty-some years ago?"

"I suppose it's possible but it does seem she considered accepting money from him at least once. But it's pure guesswork to speculate why she chose not to reply to his advances."

Dempsey was trying to instill some caution into whatever speculation I might be entertaining. I was grateful for his thoughtful attention but there were more questions I wanted to ask.

"What can you tell me of the murder arraignment and trial? I saw your name on the documents of the arraignment but not the trial."

"It was Julie who called me to tell me that Alicia was in trouble. She knew I was a casual friend. I went immediately to interview Alicia but couldn't penetrate her stupor. I stood with her at the arraignment and asked the judge to appoint a criminal lawyer to represent her. The pro bono guy was young and inexperienced but watching from the sidelines, I thought he was doing all the right things. Her guilt was obvious, her mental condition as well, and the verdict and sentence clearly a given. What do you have in mind to do now?"

I had been revolving plans in my mind while we talked.

"I believe I'll try to begin at the beginning, with Alicia's origins. My birth certificate was issued in Ulster County so that's where I'll go next. Say, can I engage you as my legal counsel in case I need one?"

"Sure," Dempsey said laughing. "Although I don't know why you would need a lawyer. But if you want, just give Bernice 25 or 50 bucks and she'll give you a receipt."

"OK," I said, scrambling to my feet. "I'll be in touch."

20

I started out the next morning to find the Ulster County Court House in a little town called DeRuyter in upstate New York. Inquiry of the Clerk of the Court for the marriage record for an Alicia Ardith Bonham brought out a huge ledger, labeled 1965-1975 and filled with handwritten entries. As the clerk spread it on the counter, she commented,

"We get lots of calls for this sort of thing these days, adopted people following up on birth parents. Sometimes I wonder if it's the wisest thing to do, but hey, my job is to serve the public, not to give it advice."

After much shuffling, we found the entry: Alicia McManus, age 18, and Roger Boyd Bonham, age 20, married on May 4, 1970. Alicia had added two years to her actual age; the R in the wedding ring was apparently Roger Bonham. They were married by a justice of the peace in the court house, only witness a secretary.

"The JP's dead 25 years ago, witness is too," the clerk volunteered, sighing in admiration. "She worked in this office till the day before she died, two days short of her ninetieth birthday."

My next stop was the library and its collection of high school year books. I found Alicia McManus in the sophomore class, dubbed the most popular girl in school, a girl with a hauntingly beautiful face, member of the choir, the pep squad, and the drama club. No

Roger Bonham was recorded in the years before or after her class. I photocopied items that featured her and added them to a file growing in my briefcase. In a current phone book I found and jotted down phone numbers for the McManus entries; if there were Bonhams in the DeRuyter area they were unlisted.

Leaving the library, I spotted a hole-in-the-wall diner across the street and decided to make lunch my next move. The décor of the diner was a brave attempt to convey the atmosphere of a country kitchen; the clumsy artlessness of the attempt cast a kind of unconventional charm over its haphazard ambience, but it was clean and its odors were appetizing. The lunch rush was over if indeed it had ever occurred. The place was empty except for an old fellow with a baseball cap and a Santa Claus beard, hunched in a back booth behind a newspaper. Seeing me take a stool at the counter, he yelled "Marge!" and a hefty woman in a blue-and-white checked gingham pinafore appeared. Her appearance was completed by a mop of suspiciously red hair confined in a hairnet and by sharp black eyes bracketed by the glitter of dangling glass earrings. Having taken my order and dispatched it to the kitchen, she returned to lean her elbows on the counter in front of me and to initiate a conversation. She seemed to be about the right age to have known Alicia McManus and so I asked.

"Alicia McManus? Hmmm? Well, no. Although I heard of her. She was hot stuff in this town, beauty and brains, they used to say. I didn't know her because I went to a different high school. You interested in her?"

"Yes," I said. "I think we might be related; my name and her married name is the same, Bonham. I'm in town tracing roots, you might say."

"Oh, Bonham. Yeah, she was married to Roger. Lord, he was a bad apple. Talk was he beat her and that's why she divorced him. I think she worked at the Emporium for a while. Pa, didn't gossip have it some guy raped her and got her pregnant? I think she left town after the baby was born."

The old man in the back booth yelled a sharp rebuke, "Marge, shut up that stuff. You know I don't hold with loose talk. Ain't the lady's order ready?"

Marge bridled and flounced back to the kitchen to bring me my tuna sandwich and a glass of iced tea. Pa's rebuke had shut off the flow of her talk. When I was in the car again, I started calling McManus numbers. The first got me an answering machine informing me its owner was out on a roof job. The second reached a harried young woman trying to talk over a background of screaming kids; she hung up on me to deal with what was clearly an infantile crisis. The third call hit pay dirt. Mrs. Henry McManus was at home and would be happy to talk with me. With her address and directions I found her neat clapboard cottage set in a lovely green lawn studded with tall old trees and fringed with bright orange marigolds. She was sitting on the porch, her considerable bulk crammed between the arms of an Adirondack chair. An elderly woman, she wore a crisp print dress; bejeweled rims on her bifocals sparkled over the plain features and deep wrinkles of her face. A pitcher of lemonade and a plate of cookies stood ready on a side table.

"Come on, honey," she invited. "Sit down and have some refreshments. I'm glad to have the company. The days drag since I don't have anybody to do for. I should tell you right off I don't know anything about Alicia McManus or Bonham other than what my dead husband Henry told me. He was a second or third cousin to her but she was gone from DeRuyter by the time I married him."

"What did he tell you about her?"

"That she was beautiful and smart. He would always say what a shame it was she married that Bonham boy. He was no good, she could've done a lot better. Henry said she'd never have married him if he hadn't got her pregnant. She was only 16 and her parents made her do it. Henry said the Bonham boy knocked her around somethin' pitiful, made her miscarry. But that gave her good cause to divorce him."

She stopped to catch her breath and take a draft of lemonade. She made a long reach to proffer the cookie plate. The cookies were very good, coconut macaroons. She continued, "In them days, they wouldn't let her back in school so she worked at MacDonald's for a while until the Methodist minister, Reverend Mr. Willhoit, hired her to for live-in help for his wife with baby tending, cleaning, and such. That is, till she was pregnant again. Henry always said it had to be rape, she was too smart to get caught again. Her folks disowned her and not long after she started to show they moved away. Henry and some other folks suspected the Reverend although no one ever came right out and said it. They just thought it because the Wilhoits stuck with her right up till she had the baby. Seemed to most folks like more than ordinary Christian charity. The Reverend's congregation idolized him and there was lots of weeping when he got moved to another parish in Illinois. Henry always said the most of it came from the ladies the Reverend counseled in his private office."

"Did you hear what came of the McManus girl's second pregnancy?"

"Have another cookie. I make 'em after my mother's recipe. Never fail. If you want the recipe, I'll write it out for you. What's that about the McManus girl? Oh, yes. Well, Henry said she had her baby, then packed up her stuff and the baby and left town. Nobody heard from her again."

I settled back in my chair pretending disinterest while I asked my next question. "I heard somewhere she went to Yonkers and got involved in some kind of scandal there."

"Well, if she did, we didn't hear about it here. We don't take much stock in what happens in the big cities on the other side of the river."

We chatted lightly for the next half hour, she wrote out the cookie recipe, and I left to ponder the day's gleanings on my drive back to Yonkers. My findings now explained the R engraved in Alicia's wedding ring, my origin, our removal to Yonkers and the absence of an extended family. Poor Alicia, on her own with a baby, no support system to rely on, so disillusioned by her experiences with Roger and the Reverend that she refused to identify a father on my birth certificate. From George Dempsey I knew she had worked hard to give me food and shelter and to supply me with treats and pleasures. And that her life, so far as he knew of it, was decent and conventional. All my childhood memories of her were loving and caring. What I was learning was leading to a really big question. Why in the world had she overdosed on street drugs and in a zombie state murdered a mother and two children? That kind of behavior seemed out of character for the Alicia I was learning about. I decided to look in the judicial documents and newspapers of the time. Perhaps there were clues to be found.

Back in Yonkers, the next day I asked Dempsey how I could go about getting a transcript of the Alicia's trial. He said he would apply on my behalf but warned me it would come at a hefty price and not for a least a week, maybe two, after the application was entered. I said OK and left him with a check and the address at my Harald home. Then I went to the newspaper office and plowed through microfiche for news of the trial, printing out all that I found. My briefcase was beginning to bulge and I began to think I had better go home. Dora's proms loomed prominently on the horizon and I knew missing them would be unforgivable. I could go over my documentary stuff at the kitchen table in a leisurely fashion while the kids were off to their summer camps.

Before I left for home, I stopped by the pawn shop Alicia had patronized. A sign on the door said "GOOCH, In business since 1944." Three balls, the traditional sign of a pawn shop, hung over the door. A fresh-faced youth viewed through a close-meshed grille behind the counter informed me his grandfather was the proprietor of the business during the period of Alicia's tickets. He could let me see records for that period but warned me they wouldn't tell me any more than the tickets did.

"Granddad and Dad are up in Lake Country fishing, won't be back till July. If you want to talk to them, come back then. I'm just holding the fort during my summer semester off from SUNY* Rochester."

I thanked the scion of the pawnshop dynasty and headed on down the road, glad to be going home. On the way, I realized I had to come up with a plausible falsehood to explain my failure to sightsee or attend shows. I settled on visits with old friends taking up all my time. The kids would buy it but of course, Eric wouldn't and he would get the truth.

I did a lot of thinking on the long drive home. Part of it had to do with the meaning of *home;* I had come to realize that I now accepted *home* as fact more than word. My life had become so much a part of the Harald family that the only home I could imagine was with them. J.P. and Marianne, Don and Dora, become almost like kin, and Eric... well, the less I thought about Eric's place in my life the better. The other topic I pondered was the incongruity of what I had learned of Alicia's life and her dreadful deed. Learning of Alicia's crime and punishment, I had tried to blot out all memory of her, including the tender parental care she had lavished on me for eight years. I never tried to substitute

* State University of New York

Julie Corbin for that parent and even as a child knew very well I would have been rebuffed had I ventured. So after they took Alicia away I grew up unloved and unloving, avoiding school friendships and meaningful adult relationships, able to tolerate the shadow of Alicia's crime and punishment only by burying all memory of her. I realized that in the last months the home and family I had found with the Haralds had opened my heart to love and self worth. As the miles dwindled down on the road to Avalon, joy and gratitude grew and glowed in my soul. I was going *home* and I would be welcomed whatever the baggage of my and Alicia's past.

21

To Dora's great relief, I was home in time to see her off to her prom with Derek in a resplendent tux and his spotless BMW. She, of course, was lovely in a strapless pale-green satin sheath, its slit skirt a fashion not entirely to Eric's liking. For the second prom the following evening, Davy arrived in a well-pressed navy blue business suit and a borrowed, perfectly restored 1964 Cadillac. Eric in a fit of indulgence had funded a second ball gown, peacock blue, its low-cut bodice redeemed in Eric's eyes by cap sleeves and a full-length full-gathered skirt. By some malign chance, each escort had provided a white orchid corsage. Don snorted and suggested careful labeling when she pressed them for keepsakes; her retort referred tartly to his gaucherie and the different colors of their ribbons. She had a good time at both functions, the one a relatively staid affair at the downtown Antlers Club with her classmates, the other at Avalon High's crepe paper-draped gym. Eric and I had stayed up late to welcome her home from each of the affairs and to hear enthusiastic descriptions of the respective bands: Frannie Cardozo and her orchestra at the Antlers and The Billygoat Rockers at the gym. As she ran off to bed, Eric and I looked at one another with a grin and said in unison, "An evening to remember!"

Eric added, "Thanks for seeing me through my little girl's first big flings. I wish Mary could have seen her too."

I was deeply grateful he had been so diplomatic in his linkage of Mary and me to Dora's special occasion. He could have said only "I wish Mary could have seen her" and left me wondering at second fiddle status. Adding "too" made the difference.

On Sunday morning, I slept late and expected Dora would have done as well, but no, there she was attending to Zorro's litter boxes while I was making coffee. The chores completed, she came to sit at the table with me to eat cinnamon rolls.

"I'm going to try coffee this morning," she announced. "It's about time to try a grownup drink, don't you think?"

I laughed and poured her a cup to which she added generous doses of sugar and milk and still made a face over the first swallow. I decided to pry a little. "Coffee for a hangover?" I asked.

"Not me, but there are some other kids maybe hungover this morning. There was liquor at the Antlers, passed around under the table. I was invited to partake but it was whiskey and I hate the taste. Avalon High's tipple was beer at the tailgate of a pickup in the parking lot. I had a sip or two from Davy's can just to be sociable, but there were other kids hitting it pretty hard. Remember Pansy, the multi-studded girl who came to my party? Her date took her home early, wiped out. She missed the fight inside." This last bit of information was imparted with a sidelong look to test my reaction.

"There was a fight?" I said noncommittally, but couldn't resist a raised eyebrow.

"Yeah, two guys—pretty well looped—started to mix it up and some others joined in, even a couple of girls. I couldn't see much of it because Davy backed me into a corner and stood in front of me until the security guard and the chaperones broke it up. I could tell he was embarrassed but he led me to a quiet table in the back of the gym and we discussed global warming until the mess got cleaned up. I could keep up with him on that because we had just finished a segment on it in class. He was a perfect gentleman all evening and saw me to the door here with a hug and a handshake. Derek by way of contrast tried to park and maul me on the way home; he almost wouldn't take no when he tried to kiss me at the door. He smelled of liquor."

I appreciated my look into two sides of teenage partying and thanked the Good Lord that Dora had the good sense and moral stamina to weather whatever arose. It soon became evident that my optimism would be tested sooner than I expected. The bird was about to leave the nest.

The Monday after prom weekend Don's and Dora's academic achievements were featured at their school's honors convocation. Don had made the honor roll for two successive semesters and graciously tolerated being smothered with congratulations and family hugs. Dora, as expected, was named valedictorian of her graduating class and was slated to speak at the graduation ceremonies the following day. The morning before the ceremonies, the dean of Hamilton College called to announce Dora's appointment to a full-tuition ten-week scholarship to participate in what Hamilton called its International Session, a summer event beginning June 3, the following Monday. I recalled her wild elation in March upon arrival of her letter of acceptance to the freshman class of Hamilton. Since Hamilton was some 175 miles away, she expected to enter in residence in the last week of August. Hamilton was a dream come true for her. In her freshman year in high school she had decided on a career in the Foreign Service and her complete curriculum for the next three years was organized to qualify her for Hamilton. The college had a fine reputation for preparation and placement of its graduates in posts for international business and diplomacy. Although this appointment to the International Session was a great honor, as a great surprise it was also something of a problem. In three days, we had to do what we had intended to do in three months, namely, get her outfitted and supplied for dormitory life.

The day after graduation Dora, Marianne, and I entered on a mad scramble. Existing wardrobe had to be mended, washed, ironed, and packed. We had to do on-line and on-foot shopping to complete the wardrobe and get the required bed linens and drapes for her dorm room. Don was co-opted to fetch and carry and shuffle boxes and bags, and with a glum look on his face to pack up books and their shared computer. Eric cancelled a meeting with a client to get her finances squared around and credit and phone cards lined up. Because the household consensus required her car to be in perfect running order before she left, J.P. started on an overhaul. Then, Oh, Woe! an essential replacement part was back ordered and the repairs wouldn't be completed by Sunday when she was due to move into the dorm. So Eric put up her stuff in the Hummer to take her to Hamilton and getting her car to her was postponed until we could work out a convenient time to do it.

Eric took Don along on the trip. Upon their return, Eric went to check on J.P.'s progress with the car, while I got a Don's eye and ear report on the trip.

"All the way to Hamilton, he lectured Dora on what a college girl should do and shouldn't do. Dora just said yes and uhhuh until she fell asleep. When we got there she was so excited with her new digs she wasn't listening to anything we said. On the return trip Dad turned the sound system up real loud and we sang golden oldies. I think he was tryin' not to cry. I guess we'll all miss her. Dora's room is real neat, built-in bed and desk; a maid comes in once a week to do the floor. She'll do fine. She gave me a list of stuff she still needed. I'm supposed to give it to you or Marianne. She says bring it when you and J.P. bring her car. Say, will you drive me to Tony Hall's house tomorrow? I got some CDs and books I forgot to return. He lives out in the country a ways. Gee whiz, I can't wait to turn 16 and get my license. Do you think Dad will let me get a car? He did Dora."

When Eric came in to share his version of the trip, Don left to tend to his animal responsibilities. Eric was wistful, his voice a bit shaky, tears close to the surface. He said,

"I didn't think leaving her there would get to me the way it did. My little girl, away at college! She's never been exposed to the rigors of real world living, never been really away from home. I've left her at horse camp for weeks without a single qualm but today seemed such a watershed. I realized how innocent and inexperienced she is now that she'll live her life elsewhere, only coming home to us on infrequent and brief visits."

He was crossing a bridge I had already traversed. Speaking from my confidence in Dora's maturity, I wasn't particularly kind when I reminded him he needed to give her more credit for character. Since his business had for years taken him away from home for a week or two at a time, his children had learned to take separation for granted and he should too. They had certainly developed admirable character traits and become worthy of his trust. Then I relented and to distract him, started to tell him about my time in Yonkers. He listened with his usual courtesy but confessed to being tired after a long day and ready to retire. When I said I was planning a return trip in July, he suggested a real talk before I went. Of course, I said. He left with a question tinged with pique.

"What about that Pattison fellow? I thought you meant to see him on book business."

When I said I ran out of time, his mood improved appreciably before I bade him good night.

22

Don and I got around to taking Tony Hall's stuff back to him on Wednesday. The Halls lived way out in the country on a gravel road that took the prize for potholes. I was driving cautiously as we were returning when Don yelled in panic,

"Stop! Stop! You got to stop!"

I immediately braked, raising a flurry of fine gravel and dust. Don flung himself out of the passenger door and sprinted back down the road. In the rear-view mirror I could see him plunging down into the weeds and reeds of the roadside ditch. He emerged clutching a small animal to his chest and came running back to the car. His burden was a bedraggled puppy, muddy and bloody, ribs showing through its filthy hide. The puppy cradled with its head pressed against Don's chest and shoulder was obviously weak but it pushed its muzzle into Don's neck and licked his chin with a long, lolloping pink tongue. It seemed to be a beagle.

"He's hurt, we've got to hurry to the vet. Look he's bleeding, poor little guy. Somebody dumped him out. He needs help."

"OK," I said as I put the car in gear and started off again. "But look again, that's a female puppy, and I agree she needs help. But the bleeding doesn't seem acute so we don't need to break any speed records."

The Harald's vet was accustomed to emergency visits. Both Cleo and Pancho were always gashing themselves on barbed wire fences.

Annual shots and neutering brought all the Harald cats and dogs in regularly and Eric ran a tab. Don was counting on that to get this little animal into care but he was troubled all the same.

"My allowance is all tapped out. I won't be able to pay. What shall I do?"

I reassured him, "I'll take care of it for the moment so don't fuss. She's a loving little thing, isn't she?" The puppy having squirmed into position to extend her licking to Don's cheek, I cautioned, "Maybe you'd better keep her away from your mouth; she may have something contagious."

Don had carried the puppy carefully into the veterinary clinic even before I got the car parked. I hobbled in after them to find the two of them already in a treatment room from which I was excluded. Half an hour later, Don emerged. Glancing at my cane, he reported.

"She's torn off the dew-claw on her left hind leg and the wound is infected and oozing blood and pus. They bandaged her up and gave her antibiotics. She's got ticks and fleas and is seriously malnourished. They want to keep her to evaluate her and test her for heartworm and stuff. They'll let me see her tomorrow, if you'll bring me back. Please...?"

"Of course." I hadn't missed that glance at my cane. I was being expected to display a fellow feeling for this hapless puppy. Fair enough, I probably could stand a reminder of my crippled state. I had been too busy to think about it recently and had missed most of my rehab appointments. I nevertheless was obliged to play the responsible adult and so I said,

"Let's get you home and cleaned up now. If you want to avoid a lot of explanations, try to get that done without Marianne noticing. You're lucky your dad is out in the woods for the rest of the week."

"You think he'll be mad? He wouldn't have wanted that poor puppy to be left hurt and starving out in the wilds. I know he wouldn't."

"What will upset him is the way you're beginning to let your heart and soul take ownership of that puppy and its problems. You know how he feels about hasty decisions and impulsive attachments."

"Yeah." Don's voice was rueful. "But maybe the vet will find a chip to get her back to her owner, or there will be a lost-dog notice in the newspaper. By tomorrow someone may have claimed her."

His face belied his optimistic words. All the way home he sat deep in thought, fingering some coins in his pocket.

The next morning I was deadheading some potted geraniums I had placed around the doorstep of The Nest when I heard Don and J.P. arguing. Don was insisting he could ride his bike to town and J.P. was forbidding him because of the distance and danger.

"What do you need to go to town for anyway?" J.P. was saying. "I'm busy today but tomorrow I can take you."

"I need a book!" Don growled.

Sensing that the beagle puppy was still a secret, I put an end to the argument by inviting Don to accompany me on a trip to the art store for supplies. The vet clinic and the art store were only two blocks apart and all smiles, Don hopped into the car while I was getting my purse and tote bag. As we drove along, I asked,

"You must have got by Marianne with that filthy shirt. Seems nobody but you and I know about the puppy rescue."

"Yeah, I ran the shirt and some pants in the washing machine as soon as I got home. Thena, I really want to get to driving soon. I know how to drive. I can take the farm car all around our place. I'll be eligible for a beginner's permit in three weeks. If Dora were home, she'd take me to apply and then ride as the licensed passenger until got my final license. I really miss her."

"Well, how about me? Will I do?"

"Gosh, yes, but aren't you going back to New York for more visits?"

"Not till July," I reassured him.

I had barely stopped the car at Tyra's shop and he was out of it and running pell mell down the street to the veterinary clinic. I went into the shop and spent nearly an hour checking out some new sketching paper Tyra was planning to stock and then went to sit in the car until Don came back. He came loping down the street and climbed in, overflowing with good cheer.

"Her name is Lucy," he announced. "The vet tech wanted to call her Moses because I found her in the bulrushes. But I said no, she's a beagle, she's spunky, and her name is Lucy! So that's what they wrote on the card on her cage. She's all de-ticked and de-fleaed, eating like a horse, and the wound in her leg is better. The vet tested her for heartworm and some other contagious diseases; he says she's very healthy and would be adoptable once she was wormed, neutered, chipped, and immunized."

"What does 'chipped' mean? I don't believe I know what that is."

"Well, they inject this computer chip under the skin on the back of the neck of a cat or dog. The chip has an ID number that can be read through the skin and the ID is registered to the owner. So, if the pet is separated from the owner and doesn't have tags, it can be identified and returned. Lucy knows me already. When I went in the cage room, she came to the bars and said 'RA RARF' to me. But then there's the bad news."

A cloud of worry and sadness came over his face and his voice grew hoarse with emotion, as he went on to say, "Doc Kline says if no one comes to adopt her by Sunday, he'll have to eoothanize her…"

"Eoothanize? What's that?"

"You know, put her down, Maybe I'm not saying it right."

"I think Doc used the word 'euthanize.' Do you know what it means?"

"Yeah, I learned about it on TV. They either give the animal a killing dose of drug or they put 'em in a closed up space and run carbon monoxide in." His voice broke and tears spilled from his eyes. "Thena, I can't stand that happening to Lucy. I got to ask Dad if I can adopt her. Will you ask for me?"

"Whoa! I don't do things like that. You ask your dad. He's no ogre and if you ask in the right way, you'll probably get the answer you want."

He brightened and hastened to ask, "What's the right way?"

"Well," I said, "he'll be home for dinner tomorrow evening. Get Marianne to fix a meal of all his favorite things and when he's mellowed out from the good food and pleasant dinner company, pop the question. Have your arguments lined up and your facts straight and I think you'll do OK."

He absorbed my advice and sat mulling it all the rest of the way home.

23

The next day, Don came over to The Nest and spent quite a long while on the telephone to the clinic, asking questions of the tech and making notes about the pet adoption process. I complimented him on his thorough approach. He grinned and retorted,

"Last night as I was going to sleep, I caught on to the way you get Dad to indulge Dora and me. The new dresses, the party.... You get Dora and me to plan our attacks, to marshal our arguments, and to grab just the right time to make a play. After we talk things over with you, your ideas always pay off. You're a pretty cool hand, you are. Thanks."

I laughed and changed the subject with new sketches of Buster and Bertha. Bill Pattison was planning a book of their own. I spent the next day on a whole portfolio of peacock poses and then went over for dinner at the main house. Eric was home and triumphant over some coup he had pulled off on his most recent trip up north. Before we said grace, Don caught my eye and gave me an unobtrusive thumbs up signal. Marianne had prepared a splendid roast of beef, mashed potatoes and *au jus* gravy, carrot coins, and a spinach salad with almonds, mushrooms, and raspberry vinaigrette dressing. The *piece de resistance* was a German chocolate cake of truly gorgeous dimensions. Eric's fork was poised over a generous slice when Don decided the time had come.

"Dad, I want to tell you about an adventure I had the other day," he began.

Marianne spoke up. "I thought something was in the wind when you proposed this special menu for tonight's dinner. You're either in trouble already or planning something that will get you in trouble soon."

Don continued patiently with the story of a puppy's rescue, its pathetic condition, our rush to Doc Kline's clinic, and the puppy's current status. Then drawing a deep breath, he took the plunge.

"Dad, I want to adopt that puppy. If you give me permission, I'll have to borrow money to fund the process. It'll take $235. Lucy has to be wormed and neutered, immunized, and have a chip put in. The rest is for board until I can take her home. If I don't adopt her, the vet will have to you-than-ize her next Monday and I just can't bear the idea of that."

Eric had continued to eat his cake while he listened attentively. The boy finished with a half-sob and a cough. He had twisted his napkin into a shapeless mass in nervous hands. His face was a mixture of hope and hopelessness. Eric had a question,

"Isn't this pretty soon after Arthur? Have you forgotten him so soon?"

Very earnestly, Don replied, "Arthur was a part of me, and still is, and always will be. But he's gone. This puppy needs me, and I think I need her."

Marianne groaned and cried out, "A puppy! We'll have to have it in the house. Puddles and messes ruining the floors. I'm not sure I'm up to housebreaking a puppy."

Don hastened to rebut her argument. "I've got a book and I can housebreak Lucy in a week, and I will. I promise you'll never have to clean up after her. Dad, you know I'm pretty good with dogs."

Eric grinned and gave the welcome words, "Marianne, let's all have a second piece of cake to welcome a young retriever into our household, even if she is female."

Now it was I who spoke up, "Not a retriever, a beagle. The vet says almost 100% beagle."

Eric's was stunned. I had to laugh. In Eric's mind the words dog and golden retriever were synonymous. But he bore up gallantly at this bit of news. Turning to Don, "A beagle," he mused. "Well, we haven't had one of them yet. I guess it's time. Bring her home as soon as the vet lets you and have him put the bill on my tab. You'll be paying for it this summer at $25 a week working for J.P. on the farm. OK?"

Don leaped out of his chair and on to his dad in a fierce hug. Eric looked at me ruefully over Don's shoulder and winked. Monday morning Eric and Don took the Hummer and went to pick up Lucy. I was fussing with geraniums again when Eric parked in the drive in front of The Nest. Don carried the puppy gently from the car and set her down on the drive, whereupon she promptly produced a puddle before galloping off to a flower bed to explore. She soon had her head buried in the ground cover with her butt and frantically wagging tail the only sign of her location. Don went into the mud room and returned with a collar and leash, a survivor of a futile attempt to teach Prince Peter to walk on a leash. He was making a start to teach Lucy that a tug on her collar meant "Come."

Eric waved with a broad grin and drove off to see clients for the next couple of days. I was on my way to borrow a strainer from Marianne and as I crossed the mud room, I saw a grimy but functional play pen set up in Arthur's corner. The floor of the pen was layered deep with newspaper and a sturdy cardboard box in one corner was padded with an old bath towel. I presumed this was to forestall the ruination of Marianne's floors. A dish of water finished off the amenities of Lucy's new home.

The next morning I was making coffee when Don came in to do the litter box chores. He was heavy-eyed and yawning, obviously had had a sleepless night.

"How did Lucy do on her first night as a Harald?" I asked.

Don groaned and ran his fingers through his hair in a gesture of desperation.

"Me and her aren't very popular this morning. She yelped and barked, and whined and keened all night, loud enough to be heard all the way to the other end of the house. Nobody got any sleep. Thank goodness, Dad wasn't home. I got to think of some way to keep her quiet before he's home again. The book says she's suffering from separation anxiety and prescribes a ticking clock in her bed, but we don't have one. Ours are all digital."

"Ah, yes, the vicissitudes of raising a puppy," I commented.

"Vicissitudes, whatever *they* are, is all the same better than euthanasia!"

The next day I went over to return Marianne's strainer and asked how things were going. She reported, laughing heartily. "Well, we slept last night. Never a peep. The quiet got me worrying and about two in the morning, I came out to see if Lucy was OK. There was Don in his sleeping bag stretched out next to the play pen and Lucy in her box, the two of them sleeping like babies. I guess there's something to this bonding business."

The longer I observed Lucy and Don and their bonding, the more I saw it as the best thing for the boy. Arthur's affection was grandfatherly, sedate, expressed by pressing his body against Don's or flopping across his feet. Lucy squirmed and wiggled, leaped up into Don's embrace and fell asleep in his lap, kissed his neck and licked his ears, or nibbled his ankles. Her boisterous affection was artless, energetic, life-affirming, just what Don needed to dispel the lingering melancholy engendered by his mother's death and Arthur's loss.

24

Now that Dora was off at college and bubbling over with news and comment in her phone calls and e-mails, a plan was hatched to have the household travel to Belleville (where Hamilton College was located) to attend the 4th of July celebration at the college. The trip would serve to get Dora's car to her. And it would get me half-way to Yonkers after the festivities for my intended return there.

June was a month of preparation. Don worked on Lucy's training in his every spare moment. She, having become fat and sassy, was soon housebroken and responding most of the time to simple commands like stay, heel, and sit. Don was worrying about leaving her to another caretaker while he was away and he wrote out three pages of instructions for Willy Murphy, the neighbor farmer who would look after the animals while we were away. Lucy had Cleo and Pancho puzzled; they recognized her as a juvenile canine and tolerated her antics but her inexhaustible energy wore them out. They were well past their puppy days and their staid demeanor was rather affronted by the nips and nibbles Lucy inflicted on their ears and tails. I spent a lot of time out of doors sketching Lucy and the peacocks and developing something of a farmer's tan while I accumulated a new portfolio that I planned to show Bill Pattison in August.

We started out the morning of July 3 in caravan: Eric's green Mercedes, Dora's yellow VW, my white Prius. Gazing at the parking lot of the McDonald's at the first stop we made on our 175-mile trip got us all laughing at Don's crack that the lineup looked like the circus had come to town. Don was in high spirits anyway; he had just achieved his learner's permit and was being allowed some highway driving in the bug under the eye of J.P. or Eric. Marianne most often drove the Mercedes, spelled by Eric or J.P.; Eric often rode with me for company, although he was usually reading the owner's manual to identify and understand the dashboard dials and screens. They fascinated him.

We arrived tired and hungry at the Belleville Comfort Inn in the early evening, ate dinner in the motel restaurant, and arranged to meet with one another and with Dora for breakfast the next morning at the neighboring IHOP. The annual Independence Day celebration was popular with Belleville natives and former students alike and the population of the town doubled as parents and friends flocked in for the fun. We had been fortunate to get accommodations for two nights at the Inn and were warned that the restaurants in town would be jammed, better be up early for breakfast.

It had been a hot day and my room was, like most motel rooms, stuffy with stale air and clammy damp from an air conditioner that had run all day and threatened to run all night. When running, it sounded like a bag of bolts dragged over a cobblestone pavement. I finally figured out how to turn it off and after pulling aside the dusty drapes managed to wrestle the window open. The evening breeze was fresh and cool and dry, and my sleep was deep and refreshing. I woke early with time for leisurely showering and dressing. On an impulse I did something I had not ventured for almost two years. I dressed in shorts! Nervously I stood in front of the full length mirror and gave myself a critical onceover. Bronzy gold hair cut into a short, wavy cap for the summer and brown eyes gazing from a nicely tanned face; the old 36-26-36 figure surviving despite Marianne's gourmet meals and my catch-as-catch-can cooking; a rust-colored polo shirt and khaki shorts—good to go from the knees up! As for knees down, knee socks did an adequate job to cover scars and the light plastic shell on my left leg. The orthotic lift in my left shoe corrected for the inch of shrinkage that leg had suffered and I had my original five-seven height back. I looked pretty good standing still and in the confidence that this was to be Independence Day, I started to leave the room.

As I turned to close the door, Dora came running across the parking lot.

"Whoopee!" she yelled. "Lookin' goo-ood!"

Reaching me, she threw her arms around me in the hug she had perfected to communicate boisterous affection without wrecking my balance. I realized then how much I had missed her spontaneous affection. Whispering in my ear, she said,

"I'm so proud of you. Got the courage to skip the long pants! Say, hey, I got a special pass so you can park your car up close for everything. The rest of the family is already at the table. I peeked in before I came over for you. Oh, it's gonna be such a great day!"

Breakfast was a true Harald meal, talk and chatter, jokes and laughter vying with the clatter of cutlery over piles of pancakes, French toast, and caddies of fruit syrups and honey. As we ate, Dora related the agenda for the day. Baseball game at 10 in the stadium, then an ox roast in the grove, followed by a stump speech by the congressional district incumbent, then free time to rest and have a little dinner before the musical performance and fireworks in the stadium!

"Isn't this summertime? Except for special programs like yours, I thought students deserted a college campus from June to September." I was remembering my own college days.

"Oh, Hamilton is a year-round school except for a holiday from Thanksgiving to New Years and a two-week spring break. Courses in most subjects are always available and if not, there's independent study or tutorials. I like it so much here and I'm going to like it more and more. This is my kind of school."

Eric grinned and said, "It better be, as much as it's costing me!"

"Oh, but Dad, it's worth every penny and you'll see, I'll do very well."

"I know, honey. But now isn't it about time to start for the stadium?" Eric said as he reached over and hugged her.

Dora joined me in my car and like a mother duck we led a procession on foot to the stadium. Hamilton's campus was typical of small private colleges and very much like the one I knew in my college days: gracious drives winding through wide grassy lawns; century-old buildings standing among century-old trees; a tradition-ridden, ivy-draped well house. Arriving at the stadium, the car was ushered into a slot smack dab in front of a flight of about 20 steps rising sheer to the main entrance. I shuddered as I scrambled out of the car but Dora merrily led me to an elevator next to the stair.

"I looked into this," she caroled. "There are three stops, ground here, first tier for field-side seats, second stop for top tier. Isn't that nice?"

It certainly was. I was one of the happiest fans in the stands. Our seats were right down front on the sunny side. I was glad I had added a broad-brimmed hat to my ensemble. An entrepreneurial type was hawking fans and rain capes. There seemed to be no risk of rain but I bought a cape to protect my arms and thighs from sunburn. Fifty cents didn't seem to be much of an expenditure to be on the safe side. My purchase was vindicated by a brief 7th inning shower and Marianne and I huddled under the cape until it was over. The day was another hot one and water and soda vendors were doing a big business. The game was exciting, an intramural contest, juniors against seniors; juniors had the largest and loudest cheering section and maybe that's why they won.

From the stadium Dora marshaled us to The Grove, a large grassy area studded with huge oak trees. You knew it was The Grove because of the rustic sign announcing it as the gift of the Class of 1912. I could imagine the students of the day, boys garbed in knickers and girls in middies, thoughtfully planting saplings to provide a shady lawn for outdoor college functions in the distant future. A soft, blue, hickory-scented haze hung under the trees and over sun-dappled picnic tables disposed here and there. The ox on this occasion consisted of chicken, beef, and pork, done on barbecue cookers that recalled the shape of antique locomotives The cookers were lined up behind a long buffet loaded with aluminum roasters filled with meats, coleslaw, baked beans, and finger food such as raw carrots, celery, and radishes. A separate table sat ready with desserts contributed by local supporters of the school. One saw just enough of the cakes, pies, and cookies coyly concealed under a gauzy cover to titillate the imagination. The crowd was just beginning to gather and Dora and Don got me settled at a table and then went off to fill my and their plates.

An ox roast was a new concept for Marianne and she delighted in it. Coming back to the table with a plate piled high, she commented,

"I can't believe how tasty and well-cooked these meats are. Why is it called an 'ox' roast? I don't see a sign of an ox anywhere!"

Eric explained that the affair harked back to an original pioneer community gathering that featured a whole beef split and skewered on a pole, hung to revolve in a pit over a bed of coals for hours. The ox roast became a traditional feature of political campaigning and the tradition continued.

Marianne was impressed. "We didn't ever have anything like that where J.P. and I come from. Us French-Canadians were never well enough off to roast a whole cow. We milked our cows, sold our bull calves, and made meat out of a pig, cut it up and smoked the pieces and made sausage, rendered out lard and so on. We would have thought this was wasteful." She shook her head in disbelief and took another big forkful of barbecue.

Later I asked Eric how it had happened that a French-Canadian couple had turned up in his household. He said he had met J.P. in Maine years before on a timber cruise. J.P. was bossing a logging crew and Marianne cooked for it. At the time, Eric's Mary was pregnant with Dora and keeping the big house that Eric had inherited from his father was more than she could handle. The farm was going to rack and ruin because Eric's growing business was taking up all of his time. Marianne and J.P. were more than willing to trade the severe winters of the Maine woods and the hard work of logging for an easier life on the Harald spread in Avalon, Ohio.

"An arrangement made in heaven," Eric said with a contented smile. "Those two became family the minute they walked in the door and Mary saw them. None of us ever looked back."

The dessert table lived up to its promise and sated with its riches, the crowd leaned back to listen to the patriotic speech. The politician was stumping for re-election from the 5th district and his oratory ranged through every cliché of political speechifying from "Give me liberty or give me death" to "I have just begun to fight" to "One small step for a man, a giant step for mankind." Most of his audience dozed through his droning for an hour and a half while the little kids in the audience played tag and tumbled in the grass, shushed by their mothers when they got too rowdy. The peroration, a fervent recitation of three verses of *America the Beautiful,* came as relief and the crowd began to disperse.

When we were back at the Comfort Inn, Eric approached me with a proposition.

"How would you like to go out to a nice dinner at The Pewter Mug? It's a charming little place I found when I brought Dora to school. We'll go from there to the stadium for the concert and fireworks."

"I'd love to. What shall I wear?" I replied.

"Oh, you women! Nothing fancy, use your own judgment."

My judgment went with a full-length flounced and flowery cotton skirt with a shell top and a lightweight sweater in case of an evening chill. I looked very well in it and Eric told me so. The Pewter Mug occupied a storefront whose interior was decorated *a la* Paris café. It featured soft music, linen napkins, and French provincial cuisine very fitting to top off an earlier fling at an ox roast. We enjoyed spinach-laced quiche, crusty bread dipped in garlic-scented olive oil, a crisp white wine, and light conversation.

Over coffee, Eric voiced a tentative question, "Have you rethought the possibility of a relationship since I last broached the subject?"

I withheld my answer until I had reviewed the successes of my day. One risk taken to wear revealing clothing, another to negotiate crowds on the difficult footing of a baseball game and an ox roast—I seemed to have weathered major physical barriers that I had avoided for almost two years. Now if I could just get over the psychological barriers in my background…. My answer to Eric was almost a yes. But what I said was,

"Ask me that when I come back from Yonkers. I intend to deal with the demons of my past for once and all. I intend either to resolve the mysteries or to deliberately put them behind me. Will your patience last that long?"

"As long as it takes, and that's a promise you can count on," he said, taking my hand.

The concert started at 7:30, anchored by *The Star-Spangled Banner* sung by a stunning black girl with a magnificent coloratura soprano voice. Dora leaned over and whispered, "Her name is Nahala. She's from Nigeria and she lives in my dorm. She's starting an internship at the Met this fall."

The concert was rich in Sousa marches and ballads of Civil War vintage. *Lorena* was done so well, it brought tears to my eyes. The fireworks were stunning (when are fireworks ever not stunning?) and Eric held my hand as we watched. When we got back to the Comfort Inn and stood at my door, he took me in his arms and said,

"I won't see you tomorrow morning since you plan to leave so early, but take this along to remember." And then he kissed me memorably.

I was so buoyed by my adventurous day that the next morning I felt up to manhandling my bags to the car. It wasn't easy but the job once mastered left me with a fine sense of achievement.

25

The trip to Yonkers was uneventful and I arrived to take up my reservation at the Ramada in the late afternoon. I had time to call Dempsey and arrange to drop in on him the next morning. Dempsey had ordered a copy of Alicia's trial transcript and had it sent to me. He had also dug out his guardianship file and sent a copy of that. Among my other activities in June, I had spent time reading those documents and matching them against those I had brought back from my original visit to New York State. I had formed a picture of Alicia's life and the official and unofficial circumstances known of her crime. I had also gained a measure of control over the emotions they roused in me.

Most of the newspaper reports made in the two days or so after the crime seemed to have been a project, if not an obsession, of a single reporter. His name was Phil Jones and his writing was sometimes lurid; but the newspaper accounts created an immediacy for those long gone events that so much concerned me. Jones's initial interview with Julie apparently took place as soon as the police had cleared away from the house. He wrote that Mrs. Corbin recounted that she had been sitting at the kitchen table reading the evening paper when about 9:30 Alicia Bonham, her lodger, stumbled in from the back porch. Alicia's clothes were soaked in blood, her bloodied hands clutched a long kitchen knife. She sat down, carefully placing the knife on the table in front of her and clasping her hands in her lap. Mrs. Corbin called the police.

Had she had any idea of what had occurred? Julie's answer was a *non sequitur.*

"All that blood…!" she said shuddering. "But it didn't even cross my mind that she might be a victim. The blood I saw was *on* her, not coming from her. I thought the police would bring medical help and they could check her out."

When Jones asked if she was afraid, Mrs. Corbin answered, "Not of Alicia. I never thought she would hurt a fly. We just sat there till the sergeant came, staring at one another. Alicia sat stone still, her face blank and white as a sheet, her eyes dead in her head."

Sergeant Depew, when interviewed, said he was obliged to learn Mrs. Bonham's identity by questioning Mrs. Corbin. After sending Mrs. Corbin from the room, he had tried to question Mrs. Bonham. He described his efforts to Jones as hopeless. Mrs. Bonham was absolutely uncommunicative, didn't answer to her name, seemed not even to hear questions directed to her, neither blinked nor changed her facial expression, maintained an upright wooden posture. The article quoted the sergeant, "In my career I've encountered a good many individuals stoned out of their skulls, but Mrs. Bonham presented a case beyond the worst of my experience." The sergeant had the ambulance crew check Mrs. Bonham and when they reported essentially normal vital signs, he instructed them to take her downtown for interrogation at the police station.

Reading this newspaper account stirred a memory. Momma and I slept in the second floor front bedroom. I was awakened that night by radio chatter from the police cars out front and by red and white flashes of light bouncing off the ceiling and walls of the bedroom. When I got up and leaned over the window sill, I saw my mother, a small dark figure escorted by a policeman, ushered to a seat in the back of a police car. Then Julie came in and told me to get back in bed and go to sleep, that my mom was going to the police station to give the cops some information. I didn't recall anything more she told me then or ever about that evening.

When patrolmen and forensic staff dispatched from the station to start the investigation arrived, the sergeant, hoping to find the source of Mrs. Bonham's dishevelment, sent men out to knock on doors in the neighborhood. Further parts of Jones's story had been pieced together from random information gleaned from talking with individual cops on the scene. In a house encountered across the alley and down three doors from the Corbin house, every light seemed to be on but knocking on the front door elicited no response. So the officer went around to the back door, found it standing ajar, and entered the kitchen, where he found a woman lying dead in a pool of blood on the floor. He immediately called the sergeant for assistance and forensics. The sergeant hurried to the scene; before entering he learned from neighbors that a woman named Marla Moffat lived in the house and that she was a divorcee with two small children. He ordered the investigators already in the house to search it; they finally came to an upstairs bedroom where by a small night light they saw a boy about four years old, and a girl about seven, lying in their respective beds bloodied and dead.

The reporter had trouble maintaining his objectivity in subsequent stories. Sean Moffat, bright and outgoing, was in kindergarten and had just mastered his ABCs. Tamara was in the first grade and already an accomplished reader for her age. Mr. Jones interviewed schoolmates and teachers for one of his byline reports. Even read 22 years later, their comments brought tears to one's eyes. Jones's interviews of Mrs. Moffat's neighbors depicted a woman living on alimony and child support, not entirely an exemplary citizen but acknowledged to be a good mother. She frequently had male visitors in and out after dark but the kids were clean and well fed. Complaints had been filed about rowdy parties featuring beer and pot but visits by the police had not led to charges. Her ex, David Moffat, was an electrician working down on the Gulf Coast; he was an infrequent visitor but was known to send presents to the kids on birthdays and holidays.

The police released a studio portrait of the Moffat family, pre-divorce. Marla, significantly overweight, dressed by Lane Bryant, carefully made up and coiffed, sat in the middle between Sean leaning against her right leg and Tamara standing at her left. Sean wore short pants, white shirt, and a polka dot bowtie. Like any 4-year-old posed under duress in front of a studio camera, he smiled grimly but gamely at the lens. Tamara was in a frilly white dress, her pony tail tied with a large bow, her broad smile punctuated by missing front teeth. The smile on Marla's pretty face seemed genuine and unforced. David Moffat, short, burly, already balding, stood behind Marla, looking uncomfortable in a sport coat somewhat too small for him; his smile seemed strained. The stiff, vertically triangular arrangement was clearly the photographer's idea of a classic family pose. All those smiles in that photograph conferred the poignancy it conveyed. One could imagine the flurry of preparation, dressing up, and admonitions for best behavior that had preceded the trip to the photographer's studio. And the pride and pleasure when the proofs were reviewed and the final choice made for the 8x12 print for framing. A separate photo of David, shot upon his arrival at the airport, showed him mopping away tears with a large white handkerchief. The caption was "Who could have done a thing like this? A grieving father asks."

No photo of Alicia appeared in the early crop of newspaper articles, but the report of her arraignment some four weeks later carried two. One had been garnered from her high school yearbook, showing the lovely young girl, popular student and cheerleader. The other, taken just before she was removed from the courtroom, pictured Alicia in profile. The woman in that picture was almost skeletal, the bones of her face jutting in sharp planes beneath a short untidy mop of badly-cut hair, an ill-fitting jail uniform bagging from her skinny shoulders. The first and only time I looked at that photo I wept uncontrollably for an hour; then I concealed it in an envelope. I did not want to encounter that face again among my papers. The text of the item was as horrific as Alicia's appearance. During the reading of the charges, she had been a mute, motionless, unblinking automaton Then she erupted into sudden violence, shouting and screaming gibberish, thrashing until her manacled wrists bled, until the judge ordered her removed from the courtroom. Her attorney entered a plea of "Not guilty by reason of mental defect" and substantiated it by reports submitted by two psychiatrists. The next newspaper photo of her showed her being led into court for the trial. She was dressed in the dark dress with the white Peter Pan collar I had found in the fiberboard suitcase given me at Woodbridge Hall. Her hair, still short, was neatly combed and she had gained some weight. Despite the poor quality of the newspaper picture, the ashen white of her complexion and frozen expression leaped from the page. She didn't look good but she looked better. That thought failed to ease the ache in my heart.

26

I had turned next to the trial transcript. The defense opened with a string of character witnesses, co-workers from her data entry job at the electric company and from restaurants where she waitressed. They painted Alicia as a pleasant acquaintance, reserved, always on time, never ill, working hard and well, and not socializing away from work. She was noted for taking shifts for nights and weekends that no one else wanted. So far as they could tell, there was no hint of drugs or alcohol in her life. Her lawyer reintroduced the reports of the psychiatrists, both of whom diagnosed paranoid schizophrenia. Since neither physician had been able to penetrate the profound withdrawal Alicia exhibited, they had resorted to extensive interviews of her co-workers and Julie to discover, if possible, evidence of behavioral disturbance prior to the crime. They found none and concluded her situation had been induced by toxic substances taken in overdose, the effects of which were now irreversible. The judge ruled that evidence and designation of toxic substances found in Alicia's body were the purview of the prosecution.

Since a deposition given by Julie a few weeks after the crime omitted the facts of the night of the crime, the judge allowed it to be admitted as evidence witnessing to Alicia's life—always working, paying room and board for her and her child promptly and in full. Alicia kept a few groceries in Julie's refrigerator and prepared simple but well-balanced meals in Julie's kitchen for the child and herself. She said Alicia's only recreation seemed to be occasions she shared with Athena: trips to the zoo, plays and concerts, movies, and such. She never went out alone or with a male friend. Julie was quoted saying, "Alicia lived for work and for the child. She said she was building Athena's college fund. She never raised her voice to me or to the child, never complained about anything."

The prosecution began with Julie on the stand with the story of Alicia's appearance in her kitchen and was followed with Sergeant Depew's testimony. Sergeant Depew described Alicia's behavior and justified his disposition of her to the police station for interrogation. He then related what he had learned of Alicia's behavior in the days and hours prior to her appearance in Julie's kitchen after the Moffat killings. He traced her from her night and day jobs over two days in which no one had noticed any unusual behavior. He traced her on the day of the murders to a bakery where she purchased breakfast sweets for herself and her daughter; to the Ticketmaster where she asked for tickets to a Pop Concert which was sold out the night she wanted; to a discount drugstore where she bought toothpaste and aspirin; and then home and a simple supper with Athena, according to Julie Corbin at 6:30. Julie had retired to her bedroom to look at TV and heard Alicia take Athena upstairs and put her to bed at 8. Mrs. Corbin dozed until she got up to read the newspaper and although Alicia must have left the house, Julie could not say when. None of the Moffat neighbors had seen Alicia then or ever entering the Moffat house, although they had seen Marla entertaining a couple of her male friends earlier in the evening. No one could describe the men other than they were tall and casually dressed, too dark to see more. The audience tittered in amusement as Depew repeated what the elderly woman next door had said when the sergeant had pressed her for more information. Did he think she spent all her time spying on Marla? She had better things to do! The prosecutor did not appreciate this bit of comic relief and recalled him sharply to the substance of his testimony.

The sergeant then related how he had subsequently managed the investigations in the Moffat house and the prosecutor called the testimonies of the individual cops who had viewed and searched the

Moffat house. The medical examiner came to the stand to describe the scene of Marla's and the children's death.

"Mrs. Moffat was subjected to a sweeping cut across the neck which transected the jugular vein; she bled to death in less than a minute. The jugulars of the children were similarly cut, with similar results."

The testimony was momentarily interrupted by an anguished cry from the back of the room. David Moffat had leaped to his feet, calling out,

"Jesus have mercy, my kids, my kids. Oh, God!"

The bailiff was dispatched to see him out to the hall and the medical examiner was instructed to resume.

"Mrs. Moffat was found to have significant amounts of methamphetamine in her blood consistent with recreational use. Her stomach contained an amount of whiskey equivalent to a couple of neat shots. No toxic substances were found in the children."

The next testimony came from the department's forensic toxicologist. Tests performed on Alicia's blood four hours after the discovery of the murders disclosed very high concentrations of methamphetamine, LSD, and stramonium metabolites,** enough to account three times over for Alicia's subsequent disorientation and permanent mental dissociation. The district attorney asked the toxicologist how the drugs might have been ingested.

"Orally, presumably as a cocktail in some alcoholic liquid. Vomitus found on the back steps of the Moffat house was also positive for these substances. Vomiting probably saved Ms. Bonham from death. The mix and concentration of the drugs found is often associated with lethal outcomes."

The district attorney asked one more question, "If you were speculating how the drugs found in Mrs. Moffat and Ms. Bonham had been acquired, what conclusion would you reach?"

"Doping parties sometimes have outcomes similar to this case—recreational ventures gone wrong. No such conclusions can be drawn in this instance. There was no sign of drugs of any kind in or on surfaces

----

** LSD: lysergic acid diethylamide, a substance often taken recreationally for its hallucinogenic effects, with potential for severe psychotic effects. Stramonium: a substance extracted from leaves and seeds of *Datura stramonium* (jimson weed), taken in some cultures in rituals for spiritual experiences, also with potential for severe psychotic effects.

of any cup or glass or any other container in the house. A thorough search of the Moffat house found no stashes. The only evidence of drugs occurred in Mrs. Moffat's blood, in the vomit, and in Ms. Bonham's blood after she was taken into custody."

27

On the face of it the case seemed open and shut; it went to the jury without further testimony and the verdict of guilty came back in less than an hour. Sentencing took place six weeks later—a life term in an institution for the criminally insane. Alicia was remanded to Woodbridge Hall. Phil Jones wrote a recap story for his paper, George Dempsey successfully petitioned the court for guardianship of the child, Athena Bonham, and Julie Corbin was designated as foster parent. And life went on.

I learned from Dempsey's guardianship file and informal notes that he moved me to a new school when the teachers in my current school complained that my presence disturbed the other children. The kids repeated things overheard from their parents, none of the girls wanted to sit next to me, boys made cracks about my "bloody momma." I had no memory of the details, even when Uncle George told me my mother's story on my sixteenth birthday. What he told me that day lay like a big, cold, hard stone deep within me, both then and for years after while I made every effort not to think of it. Sitting in The Nest's cozy living room or lying in my snug bed with Zorro draped across my ruined leg, I thought about what I had read in those old newspapers and the trial transcript. Whether I had grown up, or whether time had blunted the impact of events, or whether the peace of my present life soothed old pain, I didn't know—but in the quiet moments of the night, I felt that cold, hard stone start to dissolve. It was replaced by a growing resolution to face the mysteries, get the facts straight, and get over the anguish they caused. I meant what I said when I told Eric, "I intend to deal with the demons of my past for once and all. I intend either to resolve the mysteries or to deliberately put them behind me."

When I saw Dempsey, I asked the whereabouts of Reuben Morris, the young lawyer who had defended Alicia. Morris had gone on to a distinguished career, had formed his own law firm, and having joined the Army Reserve, was now assigned to active duty on the Judge Advocate's staff in Afghanistan. Well, that eliminated him as a subject for interview. I went on from Dempsey's office to Alicia's pawn shop. Since I had been there, a fine new sign had been installed over the front door, emblazoned with "GOOCH, Fair Pawn and Fair Dealing." The traditional three balls dangled from a bracket on its bottom edge. Inside, the man behind the wire mesh screen was an older version of the youth I had talked with the last time.

"Oh, you're the person Trey told us about," he said. "Pop's the one you want to talk to. I only got into the business 12 years ago. Make yourself comfortable, I'll call him."

While I waited, I looked around at the contents of the room on the public side of the screen. A barred case containing rifles and handguns stood against the back wall; half a dozen guitars hung beside it and a rack of eight bicycles beneath. An enormous glass-paned cupboard held shelves of tarnished silverware and art glass items. A small display case with a prominent lock contained rings, brooches, bracelets, necklaces, cuff links, tie tacks, belt buckles, and similar odd bits of male and female jewelry—none of it of any great apparent value. The hand-lettered sign propped in one corner invited an interested party to ask for a look at diamond rings. A row of antique chairs was lined up just inside the front window. Floor-to-ceiling shelves were loaded with VCRs, TV sets with screens from seven to seventeen inches, obsolete table radios, electric fans, an electric ice cream freezer. The mix of "stuff" was mind-boggling and rather pathetic—items once treasured, given up for cash, probably never to be reclaimed. My reverie was interrupted by a clatter as a door in the back opened and an elderly man in a wheel chair negotiated his way through it.

Father Gooch was a hugely fat man, ruddy-faced, with a shiny bald pate and a smiling show of large-toothed dentures over a ruff of white beard. He wore carpet slippers on his misshapen feet; swollen ankles bulged from under the cuffs of his pants. His eyes were sharp and shrewd and when he spoke, his mellow voice emerged in excellent diction. His greeting was abrupt, "You look like her, yes, you do. Sit down on one of those chairs and we'll talk."

I did as I was told and pulled out my bundle of pawn slips. "My name is Athena Bonham..."

"I know, Trey gave us your card. Your mother murdered a family in this town some years back. What can I do for you?"

"There was an accusation that my mother was a drug addict, but the small amounts on these tickets don't seem to support that."

"I can tell you she was no addict. Clear eyes, perfect complexion, decently dressed, well-spoken—we talked sometimes, she was a thoroughly nice person—just needed money."

"Did she ever say why?"

"Just needed some extra money. Said the stuff she pawned didn't mean anything to her, better to use it to treat her little girl to educational occasions than to have it lying around. Had big plans for that little girl, private school, college. Putting away every cent she could for that. Oh," he sighed, "she was such a pretty girl. When I read about her in the papers, I couldn't believe it. I always figured somebody slipped her a Mickey of some kind. You aren't hoping to redeem anything of hers, are you? Most of it sold long ago after the interest on the loan ate up its value."

"No," I said sadly. "I just wanted to learn something more about her. I was only eight when I saw her last."

"Gimme them tickets. I'll look through them. Maybe there's still something in the safe. Hey, Junior, look up number 13101, a hair clasp. Take this ticket over to him. I don't remember ever selling it."

After about ten minutes in which I sat musing and Father Gooch took a tour of his realm, Junior called out, "Here it is, Pop! Fifteen dollars. Does she want it?"

"Yes," I said eagerly, as I hurried over to the pass-through of the mesh screen. Junior pushed it toward me, a badly tarnished, antique silver hair ornament. As I held it in my hand, out of the depths of my memory I seemed to hear my mother's voice,

"We're going to *Carmen,* it's an opera. Don't screw up your face like that. These tickets cost me fifteen dollars and by golly, you're going to enjoy it."

"How much?" I asked, my voice shaking.

"Seeing it's you, $15.00. I'll write off the interest. I liked your mother. Junior, give this a lick with the polish cloth."

I limped out of the pawn shop in a happy glow. One demon vanquished—Alicia exonerated, to my satisfaction at least, of addiction and speaking to me across the years from the shiny token stowed in my purse.

28

It was with a distinct sense of unease that I pressed Julie Corbin's doorbell. I had not called to make an appointment. I hoped to catch her with her defenses, if not down, at least not on high alert. I was almost sure she could furnish missing pieces in the mystery of Alicia's madness. After several minutes I rang the bell again.

The man who opened the door to me was very tall, very skinny, more than bony, emaciated. A completely bald head, bleary yellow eyes in a gaunt face, stubble darkening his chin, matted dark hair showing through his open shirt—his appearance immediately called to my mind HIV victims I had seen in a TV documentary. His shirt and trousers looked like they belonged to a much more robust man; the belt of his pants drew slack fabric up in gathers over non-existent hips; tattered raffia sandals only partly covered his scabby feet. A wave of fetid breath engulfed me when he spoke. He swayed slightly as he stood there.

"You're Athena," he said in a raspy voice. "Spittin' image of Alicia. Come on in."

With an expansive gesture, he waved me into Julie's immaculate living room and eased himself into a chair, then continued, "Mom said you stopped in a while back. Have a seat."

"I don't think I know you," I asked. "Are you Julie's son?"

"Yeah, I'm Richard. You may not remember me. I wasn't around here much when you lived here but I knew your mother. Tried but never got it on with her."

What immediately struck me was that "Richard" might have been the R of Alicia's letters. This man, in health, might have looked to be about Alicia's age, but I had no childhood memory of him. I noticed that he was eying my cane and the outline of the cast under my left pants leg. I waited for his comment.

"Got a bum leg I see. Well, I ain't too good myself, cancer of the liver they say. That's why I'm living here with Mom. She's lettin' me since she won't have to put up with me for very long. Good thing about it, it don't hurt; bad thing, can't eat like...."

" Did you write letters to Alicia?" I interjected rudely. "From Alaska?"

"Sure, I guess so. I was up there for a while, on the pipeline. Even sent her some money, didn't have no place to spend it up there. Why're you askin'?"

I explained I had found a packet of letters signed R among her things. His eyes misted over and his voice softened. "Saved my letters, did she? Maybe she had some feelin's for me after all. Makes me feel kinda bad for what happened to her, maybe a little guilty."

"Why should you feel bad? Or guilty?"

Julie, suddenly appearing in the dining room door, spoke loudly her voice harsh,

"What're you doin' here again? I told you I wasn't answerin' any more questions. Richard don't have to answer any either."

"Oh, Ma," Richard said. "It don't make no difference now. Alicia's dead and I'm almost dead."

My breath was coming quick and hard. I gripped the handle of my cane so hard my hand hurt. I knew I must keep Richard talking. Speaking slowly and carefully, I asked, "Richard, do you know what happened the night Alicia crashed?"

"No, I wasn't there. I left the party early."

He was lying, I was sure. His gaze was shifty and his posture belied the calm delivery of his words. So I kept asking,

"What happened before you left?"

"It was kind of a welcome home..." he began.

But Julie interrupted hastily almost in a scream, "Shut up! Shut up! You got nothing to say about that night."

But Richard continued, "I been out hoboin' and just got in that afternoon and after I said hello to Mom I went over to Marla's. Her and me—well, we always got along real good and Mom told me her and Dave had split. I had some stuff I brought along from the road and I wanted to see whether she.... She had a little meth and we had some together, then Alicia came and we all had words. Alicia was always against dope. When I left, Marla was a little high but OK. Alicia was still preachin' and Marla told me to leave the other stuff, she'd try it later."

Julie stood wringing her hands, her eyes wild, her lips and heavy features working. I was still probing Richard for more information.

"Where did you do after you left the Moffat house?"

"Came over here, picked up my duffle, and hit the road again. Me and Mom wasn't gettin' along too good in them days."

As he spoke, he kept his gaze fixed on a trinket on Julie's mantelpiece, avoiding looking me in the face. I was sure the lies were covering for a lot more than the bits of truth were divulging.

I burst out, "I don't believe your story. Somehow you or Marla got dope into Alicia and what happened, happened because of it. And you left town that same night and in a hurry because you didn't want to be accountable for it. I want the truth and I'll have it if I have to sit here all day! So keep talking."

It was Julie who broke. She lifted a shaking hand to her mouth before she began abruptly to speak. "I gathered up all the money I had in the house and sent him away, told him to get out of town and stay as far away as he could get. He had a record. I was reading the paper when Alicia came in all bloody but it was 8:30, not 9:30, and Richard followed her in, white as a sheet and shaking all over. I knew I had to do something."

She sat down heavily on her stylish modern divan, planting her feet carefully side by side in the pile of the brown plush carpet, her big body sinking into the comfortable oatmeal-colored cushions. As she sat there, her arms crossed tightly across her thick chest, tense, holding herself as if she was afraid she might come apart, she rocked slightly back and forth.

29

Trying to establish some order and logic to Julie's and Richard's fragments I was hearing, I said, "Why was Alicia at the Moffat house? She didn't believe in drugs, and by all accounts didn't use them. Why would she go to a drug party?"

Richard spoke up then, "When Marla and Dave were still together, Alicia used to come over once in a while in the evening to watch a special on cable. She liked the kids although she didn't allow you to play with them—said there was too much quarreling at the Moffats. Sometimes if I was around, I visited too; me and Dave liked to talk cars. Marla didn't use meth in the house until her and Dave broke up. Alicia stayed friends with Marla after because she was trying to get her to quit—kept saying how bad it was for the kids to live with a habit. That night Alicia was just there, lecturin' me and Marla about how bad meth was for us. Marla got sort of pissed off, bein' lectured and they kinda fussed at one another."

"What do you mean, 'fussed'?"

"Talked sort of edgy. Nothing serious. After a while Alicia heard Sean call out upstairs and she went up to him; she came back saying she had told him a story and tucked him in. While she was gone, me and Marla decided to play a joke on her. I fixed up a glass of soda with some of the stuff I brought. When I had used some with guys out on the road, the buzz was kinda interesting. Good trick, Marla thought.

When Alicia drank it, she said it tasted funny but it didn't seem to do much for her. Then I had some in a whiskey and went to take a dump. I must've lost track of time in the bathroom 'cause when I came out I saw Marla layin' on the floor all bloody and Alicia layin' on top of her. I could tell Marla was dead—that godawful gash across her throat...."

Richard shuddered. Julie moaned and put her head in her hands. I swallowed hard and gathered my composure to ask, "What did you do then?"

Richard wagged his head as if trying to jog his memory, "I'm not exactly sure. My mind went all kind of fuzzy. But I think I must have picked up the knife and when Sean called out, I went upstairs and...." His voice fell to a whisper. "I guess I came back down then. Alicia was gone and I went home. She had just set herself down across from Mom and Mom was trying to get her to talk, but she was like a zombie."

Julie seemed driven to continue the story. She covered her eyes with her hands before she spoke. "I knew Richard and Alicia had been at the Moffats, and I got him to tell me what he knew. Then I said, 'You stay here and don't let Allie get up from that chair. I'm going to see what went on over there.' Oh, God, it was awful. If I had gone up and seen the kids, I would have gone out of my mind. But I knew what I had to do. I washed up all the cups and glasses and hunted for any stuff anywhere, and wiped off whatever I thought Richard or I might have handled. When I was through, I picked up the knife and took it back and put it on the table in front of Alicia. I sent Richard on his way and called the police."

When she took her hands away from her face, she looked at me with a stare of such terror and pain, I could only stare back. Recovering, I asked, "Why did you frame Alicia? For God's sake, why?"

"I thought when she woke up she would set everything straight. I knew Richard hadn't killed Marla, he didn't have one drop of blood on him. Alicia must have done it. Then when she never made sense ever again, I thought Richard was in the clear. Nobody but me and her knew he was there."

"Why did you put Richard's letters to her in the suitcase? What was that for?"

"I didn't even know they were from Richard. I don't know why I did it. I just gathered up what seemed to be keepsakes and put them in the suitcase."

"Why didn't you come forward with the truth? Did you *want* Alicia to be convicted and confined? What did you have against her?" My voice had risen and grown shrill.

"Me and Alicia weren't even friends and Richard was my son. My loyalty was to my own blood. I paid for it, didn't I? Gave you a home and raised you. Alicia's brain was ruined, wasn't it? What good would telling all this have done? She killed Marla, she didn't know up from down then or ever. I couldn't see stirring things up and maybe getting Richard in trouble."

Tears started from Julie's eyes and she held out her hands toward me in a helpless gesture—or was it a plea for mercy or for forgiveness? She went on to say, "Alicia had about $500 in the bank and I spent every cent on you, never used one penny for anything of my own. Ask George Dempsey, he'll tell you."

I sat speechless for what seemed long minutes. Richard hunched over in his chair; his next words jolted me out of my reverie. "What are you goin' to do about this? I don't see no way to go back, and no reason to try. All this is done and over, ain't it? Gettin' the law after me now won't bring Alicia back, will it? I'm about to die anyway. I don't even know whether I did anything wrong. And Mom didn't do anything so wrong the law would punish her. Can't we just let it go?"

Suddenly, I was furious and I burst into a tirade. "Innocent blood unavenged! Alicia condemned to a living death! Those slaughtered children! How can you two sleep at night, knowing how it all happened and the hand you had in it? That stuff you brought home, Richard, was a horrid mixture of LSD, meth, and stramonium—what gave you an 'interesting buzz' wrecked Alicia's brain. And Julie, when you shielded Richard, you gave the police and D.A. an open-and-shut case against Alicia. Maybe the truth told at the time wouldn't have returned Alicia to sanity, or cleared her of murder most heinous—but maybe she wouldn't have been labeled as a monster, maybe the jury that found her guilty could have considered extenuating circumstances, maybe someone would have felt sorry for her. A trick! You and Marla played a trick! Some trick! Death and destruction! I hope you both rot in hell!"

I scrambled to my feet and made my way as fast as I could out the door and down the steps to my car. I started it and put it in gear and drove a couple of blocks down the street where I pulled to the curb and stopped. The tears of rage and outrage that blurred my vision diminished into a heart wrenching flood. I wept for Alicia and twenty years of cruelly wasted life; I wept for myself cheated of my mother's gentle nurture; I wept for Marla Moffat and Sean and Tammy weltering in their blood. And I wept for David Moffat bereft of his murdered children. I sat there shaking and mopping my face with Kleenex for perhaps twenty minutes. A white-haired woman carrying a cane and walking a dog stopped and tapped on my window, mouthing a question was I all right. I reassured her with a wave and started the car again to drive away. I saw her in my rearview mirror looking curiously after me while her dog, a frowsy cocker, watered a light pole.

I went straight to Dempsey's office. The blue-haired secretary asked me to wait, he was with a client. The half-hour wait gave me a chance to regain my composure and put the Corbin information into perspective.

When I entered Dempsey's office, his first words to me were: "You've been crying. What did you find out at Julie's place?"

"Crying's all done. I've got the solution to the mystery. Maybe not all the t's are crossed nor all the i's dotted but I know what happened and that my mother was a victim, as much or more so than Marla Moffat. The Corbins came clean."

"Corbins, plural?"

I explained about Richard and told the story as I had assembled it. Dempsey listened with a sad look on his face, nodding occasionally. When I finished, he said,

"I'm both sorry and glad—sorry for the way it turned out but glad you finally know. What are you going to do about it?"

"I'm going to put it behind me and let the two of them stew in their own juice. If they put in sleepless nights wondering what steps I might take, so be it, good enough for them. I don't think they are so callous as to ignore the past, but they've done a pretty good job of shelving it for more than twenty years. I'm willing to let them think about it and worry about my next move from now on. I won't forget this horror story but I can now remember and grieve for the Alicia who was my good and loving mother until Richard and Marla's trick took away her sanity. In a warped way, it pleases me her mind was destroyed; she didn't have to understand her crime and feel her guilt every moment until death released her. In an equally warped way, I'm pleased that the guilty ones are obliged to dwell on their guilt now that it's not just their secret."

I drew a long breath and rose to my feet, saying, "I'll be leaving for Ohio tomorrow morning. Are there any bills I should settle with you before I go?"

"Nope, you're all paid up. I hardly know how to say farewell, except I hope you will really *fare well* in the original sense of the words from now on. Keep in touch. I want to know you are healthy and happy and healed."

As he accompanied me to the door to show me out, I turned and embraced him.

"Thanks, Uncle George," I said, "for the years of your faithful guardianship. I never appreciated them so much as I do right now."

30

I left for Avalon the next morning, stopping only in Belleville for a quick moment with Dora and for an overnight at the Comfort Inn. When I started out again, the day was rainy, the sun making a gallant but unsuccessful effort to penetrate gaps in the clouds. By the time I reached the Harald drive, the rain had stopped and the late afternoon sun was shining brightly. Light glinted from the wet leaves of the woodland trees; dust lay trapped in the gravel of the lane. Pulling into the parking area in front of The Nest roused Cleo and Pancho from their cozy nook at the barn. They came to greet me with a chorus of barks that woke Lucy from a snooze in the mud room. Her yelps and yips brought Marianne to the door and across the drive to hug me and help with the bags. I was HOME and as I looked around the cheerful surroundings, I realized how much I treasured them. I had called the night before to alert Marianne and she had laid in supplies and returned Zorro to The Nest. Don was helping J.P. to clean out a ditch in a distant field but I was expected to supper in the main house when they came in. Eric was not due back for another day. I slipped into jeans and a tee and flopped on the sofa for an hour's nap, with Zorro ensconced on my chest, purring like a steam engine. I woke to hear Lucy's nails scrabbling on the hardwood floor as she galloped in and Don calling out his welcome as he followed.

"Gee, I'm glad you're back. I've got so much to tell you. Seems like you been gone for a month! Hurry over for supper. I'll be ready to greet you right and proper as soon as I shower and change clothes. Bush hogging is hot, sweaty, dirty work." And out he went, Lucy tearing along behind him.

At dinner, Don held center stage, relating his adventures with Lucy who had added several accomplishments to her repertoire: She now knew "bed" and "out" and there had been no untimely or untoward eliminations for two solid weeks. Marianne was pleased to confirm this bit of news. J.P. reviewed the work on the farm and Don's important contributions to it, despite a case of poison ivy and a crop of blisters acquired the first day he worked on the ditch. Don beamed when acknowledging J.P.'s compliments. Marianne had forced him to slather himself with SPF 110 (the number Don's hyperbole conferred on his sunscreen) and consequently his arms and face had tanned handsomely. I suspected he had donned a snow white tee shirt for dinner wear just to show off his tan. He also related jubilantly that Eric had promised to take him to look for his own car Saturday next. He had run down by the time dessert came to the table and two pieces of peach pie had disappeared under his flying fork. I excused myself early. Despite my stop in Belleville I was tired from two days on the road. Once in my comfortable bed, I slept dreamlessly and woke ready to wrestle my weight in wildcats.

I spent the morning—not wrestling wildcats—but organizing my art supplies for an attack on the demands of the new book. Don had inquired politely if I had met with Bill Pattison while I was in New York and concealed a gleeful grin when I said I had had no time. He turned glum again when I informed him that Bill was expecting to drop in on a visit to Avalon the first week of September.

Eric called at noon. "Prepare to dress up. I'm taking you out to dinner as soon as I get home and complete some serious grooming. I should be at your door at 7 P.M. And before you ask me what you should wear, I'll tell you—your best evening duds. Whaddya say?"

"I say, great! I'm looking forward to seeing you."

"Does that mean your visit to Yonkers was a success?"

"More or less. I'll tell you about it."

After signing off, I headed for the closet. My favorite gown, a gauzy glowing tropical print, needed a touchup with the iron to restore the "swish" to its full-length skirt. My vicuña shawl, a fashion once worn by Inca nobility and for me a souvenir of a shopping foray to an exotic bazaar in Peru, had to be refreshed in a steamy bathroom. A heavy gold necklace and dangling earrings, acquired in another exotic bazaar, this one in Nairobi, completed the ensemble—with the exception of shoes. I never resented the paraphernalia required by my damaged left leg so fiercely as when I was facing a first class dress-up occasion. Shoes of shiny gold leather studded with fake gems can be bought, but when constructed or modified to compensate for my disability, they fail miserably as a fashion statement. In a word, they look godawful. So I sat for a long minute on the edge of the bed, gritting my teeth, telling myself insistently that the long full skirt would disguise my footwear. Away with female vanity, my common sense counseled and finally prevailed. By 6:55 I had resigned myself to ignoring my feet while preening over the rest of my garb. I was rather taken aback when the seldom-used door bell rang. Eric must think this a formal occasion calling for a formal entry at the front door.

I opened the door to find him in an smartly tailored dinner jacket. He whistled by way of greeting, then said admiringly,

"When I said dress up, I didn't mean you had to look like a million bucks. But here you are, looking like something more than a million. Wow!"

Suddenly it no longer mattered that my shoes were ugly. I felt thoroughly beautiful as Eric handed me into the Mercedes. As we traveled to the restaurant I considered introducing the news from Yonkers into a lull in our conversation but none seemed suitable. Dinner was at Soir Provençale, a palatial house in Mediterranean style, set among formal gardens. Eric said it was originally built for a magnate grown rich from the manufacture of rubber tires at the dawn of the automobile age. We were seated among fashionably dressed people murmuring at tables in what had been a drawing room; a string trio played softly. The light from crystal chandeliers and sconces reflected from fine china, silver, and stemware arranged on fine linen. With Eric's discreet hand on my elbow and my cane firmly in hand, I achieved a not ungraceful entry over handsome Oriental carpets. I am not such a country hick that I have never dined in sophisticated surroundings, but this beat anything in my past experience. The scene seemed like a 40s movie set with Cary Grant about to make an entrance. Settled in my chair, I prepared to enjoy the luxury. A *sommelier* recited the wine list and I relaxed my abstinence from alcohol to indulge in a light champagne. Seven courses later, among them a *langouste* which our waiter assured us had slept in the Mediterranean only 24 hours before, I was a little giddy and we were replete with food so fine it beggars description. I had almost responded to one of Eric's quizzical glances between courses by initiating the Yonkers story but the time and place didn't seem right. Instead, I enjoyed watching Eric's handsome face bent seriously over the job of disassembling his shellfish. I had the waiter de-construct mine; unaccustomed as I was to alcohol these days, his assistance was essential.

An ornate tall clock was striking eleven in mellow tones when our waiter asked, "Will you have coffee here or in the conservatory?"

"It's a warm evening, maybe the terrace would be nice." Eric ventured, only to be shot down by the waiter who said he couldn't recommend it, mosquitoes he whispered. So we had our coffee enthroned on the plump cushions of a settee under the drooping leaves of a gigantic banana tree while stars sparkled through the glass roof. Incredibly, the surroundings had made us both self-conscious and inhibited the usual free flow of our conversation. I decided the time and place for real talk was The Nest and I finally took the bull by the horns.

"Let's go home," I said abruptly. "This is all very nice but …."

Eric sighed his relief and hastened to agree. Back in the Mercedes and bowling along the highway, Eric removed his tie and we sang golden oldies. At The Nest, Eric plugged in the coffee pot while I changed into slippers and shed my heavy jewelry. We ended up on the sofa, smiling comfortably at one another. Eric was rueful.

"I'm sorry. I planned this evening to be a gala occasion. Somehow I feel like it fell short for both of us."

I chuckled and reassured him, "It was a great evening, wonderful food, wonderful surroundings. I will treasure forever the sight of you dealing with that big lobstery thing. You made eating it a triumph of mind over matter!"

He threw back his head in a hearty laugh. "I thought I'd never get through that shell, and that tiny fork…well, did you think I was a total rube?"

"Not at all," I said very seriously. "I was admiring a man showing grace under fire. You are a very admirable guy, you know, and not just in difficult situations."

"That's the first compliment I've ever had from you and the most heartwarming I've ever had from anybody." He reached for my hand as he smiled. "Is this conversation slated to progress as warmly as it has begun?"

I took his hand in both of mine and looked him straight in the eye. We were in the right place and the time was now. "I'll let you judge the quality of the conversation after I have brought you up to date."

I sketched in the background of newspaper and trial information that I had assembled. Then I related my conversation with Richard and Julie Corbin.

"Richard didn't admit to killing the children and if he did, maybe he doesn't remember it. I will always think he did. But it's not unbelievable that Marla's death was an accident at the hands of Alicia and that Richard, his mind warped into madness by the same drugs, did in the children as a cover up. I've decided it doesn't matter if I don't know the Who or What or How. In my mind, I have absolved Alicia. She's the only one who has ever mattered to me. She was a victim from the time Roger Bonham courted her till her heart wore out in Woodbridge Hall. She was young and attractive and whole until Roger betrayed her first love. I don't care whether Reverend Wilhoit was or wasn't my biological father. I only grieve that another man betrayed my mother. That betrayal had a good part, it gave me life. Alicia loved me as long as she was capable of it, she saved every cent she could toward my future, she pawned her pitiful possessions to give me occasions to remember. I told you I loved *Fantasia*, well, I have since remembered she took me to see it as a child and we laughed together as we watched that hippo ballet. Maybe now that I have no reason to feel shame and humiliation and infamy when I think of my mother, I will be able to remember more of the happy times I spent with her. I'm free of the demons who have lurked in the shadows of my mind for so many years."

Eric put his arm around my shoulders and bent to kiss my hand. I snuggled gratefully into the warmth of his embrace. We sat quietly for several minutes before he spoke, "Aren't there more demons to exorcise? Seems to me I've run into them a couple of times before now."

"All right. The remaining demons are epitomized by the scars and cast that decorate my left leg. The surfaces have healed but the deep hurt persists. I was lovely and perfect until three years ago, overflowing with health and *joie de vivre*, mentally and physically agile. I concede my brain works as well as ever, and perhaps my talents have actually grown. I admit I still have most of my looks, but I'm damaged goods, handicapped and crippled, irrevocably and as long as I live. Knowing that corrodes my sense of self. I'm still not sure it won't corrode relationships with people I love. I'm afraid to take the risk. Once I commit, I want to love and be loved forever. "

I fell silent. Eric pulled me around to face him and exploded with bottled up frustration and anger. Red-faced, eyes flashing fire, he said, "That's a crock and you know it! Where's the girl who resolved never to whine or complain? But here you are whining, feeling sorry for yourself. I know you have days and nights when pain drags your spirits down. So far, however, I haven't seen you turn low spirits into bad temper or abuse of Zorro or me or either of the children or Marianne and J.P. You seem to be able to put your stress aside from the relationships you have in this household. You are loved, you hear me, *loved* by each of us, you are a treasured friend, not some medical case to be pitied. Now I'm laying down the law. Hear the law according to Eric Harald. Are you listening?"

I nodded, numb, a little frightened, wondering what was coming next. Then his tone grew tender as he continued. "I'm not like the others who love you. I love you as a man who loves a woman and wants to share life with her. I intended to ask you to marry me this evening over our gala dinner. Too bad we got too self-conscious to speak out. I think this is a better time and place anyway."

He fumbled in his shirt pocket and pulled out a small velvet box.

"Don and Dora helped me pick it out several months ago. They gave my proposal their blessing and they've been badgering me ever since to pull it off. Here," and he flipped open the box lid. "Let me put it on, will you?"

Nestled in the cushion of the box was a white gold band with three diamonds mounted in a cluster. Impulsively, I put out my hand and Eric slipped the ring on my finger. "The kids wanted me to make sure you knew the three stones meant you would be marrying the three of us. Is that OK? Oh, for God's sakes, don't cry!"

But I did anyway and Eric had to get up and go for the roll of paper towels from the kitchen. The resignation on his face tickled me and my chuckle stopped my tears.

"Why do women have to get so emotional and cry over everything?" he grumbled. "Come on, I want to see you smile! I want to hear you laugh! I want you to look happy!"

THE LAST AND
BEST CHAPTER

I smiled and laughed and looked happy, then and from then on. I'm still smiling, jolted out of self-absorption and into the love I had tried to ignore. I was smiling when we broke the news over dinner the next evening. Marianne hugged me until we were both breathless. J.P. shook my hand, then shook it again, grinning like a marionette. Don let out a whoop of triumph so loud Lucy thought she needed to add her best yelp and howl to the bedlam. I was smiling when we called Dora and told her. She immediately began planning a wedding to be held in the family and living rooms of the Harald house during Hamilton's winter holiday. I was even smiling and laughing when Lucy, a big white bow tied to her collar, chased Prince Peter through the wedding ceremony. It's easy to smile when you have the love of your life by your side. My imperfect body doesn't bother me or anyone else any more. That's another effect of real love.